This book
belongs to

_____

_____

HENRY HOLT LITTLE CLASSICS
THE BEST OF BOOKS FOR CHILDREN
ILLUSTRATED BY CONTEMPORARY ARTISTS

ROBERT LOUIS STEVENSON
TREASURE ISLAND
illustrated by Colin McNaughton

LOUISA M. ALCOTT
LITTLE WOMEN
illustrated by Michael Hague

EDWARD LEAR
NONSENSE SONGS
illustrated by Jonathan Allen

ANNA SEWELL
BLACK BEAUTY
illustrated by Victor Ambrus

THE BROTHERS GRIMM
FAIRY TALES
illustrated by Amanda Harvey

other titles in preparation

FAIRY TALES

The moment he kissed her she opened her eyes
(Rose-Bud)

THE BROTHERS GRIMM

Fairy Tales

selected from the English translation by
EDGAR TAYLOR

illustrated by
AMANDA HARVEY

HENRY HOLT AND COMPANY · NEW YORK

Henry Holt and Company, Inc.
Publishers since 1866
115 West 18th Street
New York, New York 10011

Henry Holt is a registered
trademark of Henry Holt and Company, Inc.

Design and typography copyright © 1994 by Pan Macmillan Children's
Books
Illustrations copyright © 1994 by Amanda Harvey
Introduction copyright © 1994 by Naomi Lewis
All rights reserved.
Library of Congress Cataloging-in-Publication Data

ISBN 0-8050-3127-8
First Published in 1823
This edition first published in the United Kingdom
by Pan Macmillan Children's Books
First Henry Holt Little Classics edition, 1994

Printed on acid-free paper in Singapore
10 9 8 7 6 5 4 3 2 1

CONTENTS

LIST OF PLATES

INTRODUCTION

LATE in December 1812 a small book, *Kinder und Hausmärchen (Children's and Household Tales)*, by the brothers Grimm, was published in Berlin. It was not taken very seriously by the critics; indeed, at the time, a publisher was none too easy to find. Yet, with the added stories in later editions, it was to become a supreme bestseller, translated into some seventy languages, and one of the most influential works of the past two centuries. The first English version, Edgar Taylor's *German Popular Stories* appeared in 1823, with splendid Cruikshank illustrations. The stories here are based on Taylor's rendering.

Who were the brothers Grimm? Jacob (1785–1863) and Wilhelm (1786–1859), oldest of six (five surviving boys and a girl), were born at Hanau in Hesse, where their father was town clerk. With only a year between them, the two were as closely allied as twins, not only as children and students but – in thoughts, tastes, views, ideals – for the whole of their lives. Even Wilhelm's marriage did not end their habit of working together. Yet there were differences. Jacob, intense and tireless, was the more serious of the two. Wilhelm, whose health was less certain, was the more romantic and imaginative. When a phrase in the stories has a poetic ring, the hand of Wilhelm is very likely there. A third brother, Ludwig, known as Louis (1790–1863), was to make his name as an artist; he would illustrate later editions of the *Hausmärchen* (the 1812 edition had notes but no pictures).

In 1771, the father was appointed district magistrate of Steinau and the family moved to a large house with farmland and countryside near at hand. But the father's death brought this pleasant time to an end: no more large houses; no more tutors and servants. Jacob, now eleven, felt that he must take on himself the care of the family, a charge that stayed with him always. An aunt arranged to send Jacob and Wilhelm to the high school in Cassel. They were at first looked down upon by rich and

well-born classmates; but each Grimm headed his
class-list when they graduated in 1802 and 1803.
Now Jacob applied to enter Marburg university.
Again there were difficulties; the first places went
to students from the seven 'acceptable' social ranks.
For all their father's professional status, the Grimms
were only in the eighth. But, through useful
friends, they crossed that threshold too, each at the
age of seventeen.

And here they found good luck. Carl von
Savigny, a young lecturer in Roman law, soon
perceived that he had two students who were
not only of unusual quality, but who shared his
passionate interest in the national past. He gave
them access to his own library and brought them
into his own circle of friends. For the Grimms, the
most significant of these were the patrician Achim
von Arnim and Clemens Brentano, who were
jointly preparing a book of old German folk songs,
ballads and nursery rhymes. This, *Das Knaben
Wunderhorn* (*The Boy with the Magic Horn*), was
published in 1805, and the Grimms willingly helped
to find material for the next edition. But they were
also starting on a quest of their own, for folk tales,

never yet in print, and soon to be lost as the storytellers died and were not replaced.

At this point the tale takes a curious twist. In 1809 Brentano, intrigued by the brothers' diligence, asked if they would let him see the tales they had so far collected. They readily lent the manuscript but, perhaps with their friend's mercurial nature in mind (he was not above adding a little invention to his texts), they prudently made a copy. It was worth the labour, for Brentano never returned the forty-nine tales. Well over a century later, in 1920 to be exact, they turned up in an Alsace monastery, the Abbey of Oelenburg. A mystery indeed! But the recovered texts have a particular interest in themselves. The drafts were still in their earlier rough form, so they give a rare view of the brothers' working methods.

To find material, the Grimms alerted all their friends and contacts. One source was 'old Marie', housekeeper to the large Wild family, neighbours and friends of the Grimms' younger sister Lotte (Wilhelm would one day marry Dortchen Wild). From Marie came, among other tales, 'The Robber Bridegroom'. An old soldier, J. P. Krause, a former sergeant of the dragoons (he was sixty-four when the Grimms found him), traded stories for cast-off clothes. From him came 'King of the Golden Mountains' and (probably) 'Old Sultan'. In 1809 Jacob wrote to a student friend, now a magistrate, asking him to note down thieves' slang, under-world catchwords and superstitions. Had anyone contact with fishermen, charcoal burners, peasant women? Stories must be there. But the greatest find, in 1812, was Dorothea Viehman who came to be known as 'the Fairy-Tale Wife'. As an inn-keeper's daughter, on the highway from Frankfurt-am-Main to North Germany, via Cassel, she had listened to carters, traders, travellers, soldiers, and had a fund of tales which she told clearly and carefully, scarcely ever varying the words. Some twenty of hers are in the second book of the Hausmärchen. Louis's striking portrait of her was used as a frontispiece.

The Grimms urged always that the tales should be taken down exactly, ramblings, repetitions, crudities, just as said. The problem, though, in a book for the general reader, was to find a way of presenting this often ragged material on the printed page, restoring sense without losing the storyteller's voice. How well they succeeded can be seen anywhere in the stories here, different as they often are from one another. Read, say, the opening pages of 'The Golden Bird', and you must marvel at its economy, pace and magic. The haunting note of 'Jorinda and Jorindel' is like nothing else in the book, yet the pace and words of this matchless tale never go beyond the bounds of traditional storytelling. The solution came, it seems, when Arnim passed on to the brothers two stories told by a Pomeranian fisherman: 'The Juniper Tree' and 'The Fisherman and his Wife'. In these tales the Grimms saw the model they needed, and the path ahead was clear. Even so, they were never wholly satisfied. In later editions of the tales Wilhelm, the more literary of the two, continued to revise and change in his search for the perfect sound.

Any reader will soon perceive that the tales are not single absolutes; one crosses into another; they have their own history. Clearly their journey into the printed text has been a wandering one, through who knows what in place and distances. The Rip van Winkle theme in 'Peter the Goatherd' is even more familiar in Irish and Scottish tales. Spend a night or a week in the land of Faery and you'll find that a hundred years have passed. The theme of Beauty and the Beast – best known to us through courtly French Perrault – appears in several Grimm stories; one instance here is the superbly told 'The Lady and the Lion'. But this is also close in its detail to the Scandinavian 'East of the Sun, West of the Moon'. The Grimms' 'Hansel and Gretel' is a charming variant on the usual version; no witch, no oven. More familiar elements are in 'Roland and May-bird', yet this too has differences. 'The Seven Ravens' might seem to readers a recasting in one tale of 'The Wild Swans' and 'The Three Bears'. As for Cinderella, one of the most peripatetic of fairy tales, you will still not find the exact Perrault version in Grimm, that original was too literary – and too French. Still, in 'Cherry or the Frog Bride' six large rats are seen to draw a pumpkin coach. 'Ashputtel' offers a nearer version, though the dropped slipper is made of gold, not of glass. There is, by the way, a fairly close version in the Arabian

Nights. The famous ball, however, is attended only by men; the women have a party in their own quarters. But the girl does drop an ankle ring.

To the Grimms, the tales held clues to ancient laws, beliefs, the codes of bygone life. They were a special road into the past. But readers today are more allied to the listening peasants than to the scholars. True, the stories came from a time (not so far away) without radio, television, cinema, telephone, music available at a touch, air flight, railways, motor cars, or any other transport other than the horse or the human foot. Add your own: the list is endless.

In fairy tale, all is possible. You have the freedom of the skies, you can instantly move over distances. The poor, the orphan, the drudge, the penniless youngest son (the oldest gets the inheritance) can take the story's centre, gain the prize. Given average looks and yellow hair any poor village boy or girl can win a prince or princess. Animals talk and advise. Why not? Your enemies lose in the end and get their just deserts (a dream desire that will never be out of date). Chesterton remarked, after hearing youthful criticisms of

Maeterlinck's *The Bluebird*, 'Children, who are innocent, love justice. Most adults are wicked and want mercy.' Morality is simple and direct – there is little or none of the religious admonitory note that we find in Kingsley, Macdonald, Andersen (not Carroll) great images though they are (add, of course, C. S. Lewis, a particularly wilful example). The power of the great invented masterworks is not lessened by this content, yet the older straight good/bad ethic problem makes more impact on the young.

But, as well as its gifts, and closely linked to their workings, magic has its laws. Beware of neglecting them! The most boring of books – if they ever reach print – come from would-be fantasy writers who ignore this truth. Most rules are simple enough; show kindness and courtesy to bird, fish, spider, crone or beggarman in your path, and one or more will reveal the secret, come to your aid when you are faced with impossible tasks. Be rude and mean (the bad are always incredibly stupid in these matters) and you will get the shower of pitch, the stones you thought were gold. You won't have to look far in this book for instances. In invented stories using this motif the best, I'd say, is Ruskin's 'King of the Golden River'. Courtesy is an interesting concept in a peasant story. But it matters. Nothing in behaviour is ever wasted in a fairy tale.

Still, the most valuable magic offering is the one at the core of most stories, all the world over – the wish. Even nursery rhymes can be hidden wish songs. In, say, 'Lavender's Blue', a toiling farmboy day-dreams that he is king and his girl, another farm servant, is queen. What will they do? Sit in comfort and get the others to work. Make your wish with care! It may come about and in ways you had not foreseen. Besides, you cannot wish beyond your own capacity. What do lottery winners do with their sudden wealth? And is there any better demonstration of this than 'The Fisherman and his Wife'?

There is something more. The landscape of the mind is planted early; whatever enters then will remain through life. Deep in the mind of one-time fairy and folk tale readers are mountains, forests, distances (as well as some useful behaviour guidelines). Perhaps the most powerful and abiding is the forest – in which, in the words of Edward Thomas, at some time 'all must lose their way . . . soon or late, they cannot choose.' Thomas knew trees and woodland, but the forest in his great poem 'I have come to the borders of sleep' must come from fairy tale. A century before, Coleridge reflected: 'From my earliest reading of Faerie Tales and Genii &c &c my mind has been habituated to the Vast. . .' Though, in his characteristic way, he extended this thought into philosophic regions, his concept of the Vast must have taken in oceans, caverns, woods and mountains – all reappearing in his poems.

All folklore grows out of human needs, desires, dreams and basic happenings. Yet it is also shaped by climate, landscape and human temperament. Nearest to nature – sun, moon, wind and stars – are the aboriginal tales. The Middle East (which has genii but no fairies) typically sets its tales in the heat and chatter of bazaar or market place. The English, with no extremes of scene and weather, have produced mainly tales of a homely quality: teasing fairies, foolish giants, with cunning peasant-boy Jack as the basic hero. But mermaids might be found on the sea borders. Some of the most soaringly wild stories came from old tsarist Russia, with its bitter poverty and oppression, it's snow-bound winters and awesome scenery – forests, lakes and mountains. Germany, another such peasant country, with its wild scenery and winter cold, its mosaic of little kingdoms and principalities, was a natural seed-bed of story, as this book shows. There is coarseness and cruelty too in some of the tales as originally told (as there would be in the human tellers and listeners), but these things do not always survive translation or retelling. What cannot be lost is the intrinsic magic and poetry.

A few groups of fables and fairy tales – almost all from the French or French versions – were in German print at the start of the Grimms' century: Perrault's, d'Aulnoy's, La Fontaine's, the Arabian Nights. But there was no matching the *Hausmärchen* in power and range of story, people and creatures, quite apart from the sheer quantity. Yet had they not been rescued they would have disappeared. Today there must be few people in the western world – and beyond – who have not met (through whatever medium) the main stories. The Grimms achieved much more than they planned. Their work inspired the great collecting fervour of folk tale and folk song in nineteenth-century Europe and throughout the world thereafter. So, if less directly, are they behind the flowering of the invented fairy tale of the middle and later nineteenth century and the second flowering a century later, of writers such as Tolkien and Le Guin. Grimm may be their ancestor but they have made their own contribution to myth. No book has ever set out more skilfully the place of magic in human life, its power and limits, as well as the force of the secret name that everything possesses, than Le Guin's *A Wizard of Earthsea*.

The *Household Tales* were not the only works of the brothers Grimm. Jacob was to publish twenty-one books (mostly learned works on language, law, grammar, mythology, legend and literature), Wilhelm fourteen, and a further eight were jointly written. They also wrote numerous essays, letters and articles. Yet they had little chance of continued tranquil scholarship in the turbulence of their times. A post held under one authority would be lost in another political change. Jerome Bonaparte, whom Jacob served as a private librarian during the Napoleonic occupation, proved a more

relaxed and amiable employer than the later Elector
Ernst August, one of the many unattractive sons of
England's George III. The brothers' final posts were
professorships at Berlin University. Both Grimms
were held in national honour before they died.
(There is a fairy tale neatness in the fact that
Wilhelm's son was to marry Achim Von Arnim's
daughter).

When the Grimms began collecting they saw
their finds as a shining road into the past. They did
not realize that they were also driving a shining
path into the future. With its truth to human needs
and wishes, and its timeless telling, how can the
genuine fairy tale ever be out of date? The best of
the new myths join this road. 'The Pot of Soup',
wrote Tolkien, 'the Cauldron of Story, has always
been boiling, and to it have continually been added
new bits, dainty and undainty'. Yes indeed, The
Grimms' road into the future has reached our time
today. We need not doubt that it winds off into all
tomorrows where there are readers and listeners.

NAOMI LEWIS

HANS IN LUCK

HANS had served his master seven years, and at last said to him, "Master, my time is up, I should like to go home and see my mother; so give me my wages." And the master said, "You have been a faithful and good servant, so your pay shall be handsome." Then he gave him a piece of silver that was as big as his head.

Hans took out his pocket-handkerchief, put the piece of silver into it, threw it over his shoulder, and jogged off homewards. As he went lazily on, dragging one foot after another, a man came in sight, trotting along gaily on a capital horse. "Ah!" said Hans aloud, "what a fine thing it is to ride on horseback! There he sits as if he was at home in his chair; he trips against no stones, spares his shoes, and yet gets on he hardly knows how." The horseman heard this, and said, "Well, Hans, why do you go on foot then?" "Ah!" said he, "I have this load to carry; to be sure it is silver, but it is so heavy that I can't hold up my head, and it hurts my shoulder sadly." "What do you say to changing?" said the horseman; "I will give you my horse, and you shall give me the silver." "With all my heart," said Hans: "but I tell you one thing – you'll have a weary task to drag it along." The horseman got off, took the silver, helped Hans up, gave him the bridle into his hand, and said, "When you want to go very fast, you must smack your lips loud, and cry 'Jip'."

Hans was delighted as he sat on the horse, and rode merrily on. After a time he thought he should like to go a little faster, so he smacked his lips, and cried "Jip". Away went the horse full gallop; and before Hans knew what he was about, he was thrown off, and lay in a ditch by the roadside; and his horse would have run off, if a shepherd who was coming by, driving a cow, had not stopped it. Hans soon came to himself, and got upon his legs again. He was sadly vexed, and said to the shepherd, "This riding is no joke when a man gets on a beast like this, that stumbles and flings him off as if he would break his neck. However, I'm off now once for all: I like your cow a great deal better; one can walk along at one's leisure behind her, and have milk, butter, and cheese, every day into the bargain. What would I give to have such a cow!" "Well," said the shepherd, "if you are so fond of her, I will change my cow for your horse." "Done!" said Hans merrily. The shepherd jumped upon the horse, and away he rode.

Hans drove off his cow quietly, and thought his bargain a very lucky one. "If I have only a piece of bread (and I certainly shall be able to get that), I can, whenever I like, eat my butter and cheese with it; and when I am thirsty I can milk my cow and drink the milk: what can I wish for more?" When he came to an inn, he halted, ate up all his bread, and gave away his last penny for a glass of beer; then he drove his cow towards his mother's village. The heat grew greater as noon came on, till at last he found himself on a wide heath that would take him more than an hour to cross, and he began to be so hot and parched that his tongue clave to the roof of his mouth. "I can find a cure for this," thought he, "now will I milk my cow and quench my thirst;" so he tied her to the stump of a tree, and held his leathern cap to milk into; but not a drop was to be had.

While he was trying his luck and managing the matter very clumsily, the uneasy beast gave him a kick on the head that knocked him down, and there he lay a long while senseless. Luckily a butcher soon came by driving a pig in a wheelbarrow. "What is the matter with you?" said the butcher as he helped him up. Hans told him what had happened, and the butcher gave him a flask, saying, "There, drink and refresh yourself; your cow will give you no milk, she is an old beast good for nothing but the slaughterhouse." "Alas, alas!" said Hans, "who would have thought it? If I kill her, what will she be good for? I hate cow-beef, it is not tender enough for me. If it were a pig now, one could do something with it, it would at any rate make some sausages." "Well," said the butcher, "to please you, I'll change, and give you the pig for the cow." "Heaven reward you for your kindness!" said Hans as he gave the butcher the cow, and took the pig off the wheelbarrow, and drove it off, holding it by the string that was tied to its leg.

So on he jogged, and all seemed now to go right with him; he had met with some misfortunes, to be sure; but he was now well repaid for all. The next person he met was a countryman carrying a fine white goose under his arm. The countryman stopped to ask what was o'clock; and Hans told him all his luck, and how he had made so many good bargains. The countryman said he was going to take the goose to a christening. "Feel," said he, "how heavy it is, and yet it is only eight weeks old. Whoever roasts and eats it may cut plenty of fat off it, it has lived so well!" "You're right," said Hans as he weighed it in his hand; "but my pig is no trifle." Meantime the countryman began to look grave, and shook his head. "Hark ye," said he, "my good friend; your pig may get you into a scrape; in the village I just come from, the squire has had a pig stolen out of his stye. I was dreadfully afraid, when I saw you, that you had got the squire's pig; it will be a bad job if they catch you; the least they'll do will be to throw you into the horsepond."

Poor Hans was sadly frightened. "Good man," cried he, "pray get me out of this scrape; you know this country better than I, take my pig and give me the goose." "I ought to have something into the bargain," said the countryman; "however, I will not bear hard upon you, as you are in trouble." Then he took the string in his hand, and drove off the pig by a side path; while Hans went on the way homewards free from care. "After all," thought he, "I have the best of the bargain: first there will be a capital roast; then the fat will find me in goose grease for six months; and then there are all the beautiful white feathers; I will put them into my pillow, and then I am sure I shall sleep soundly without rocking. How happy my mother will be!"

As he came to the last village, he saw a scissor-grinder, with his wheel, working away, and singing

> O'er hill and o'er dale so happy I roam,
> Work light and live well, all the world is my home;
>   Who so blythe, so merry as I?

Hans stood looking for a while, and at last said, "You must be well off, master grinder, you seem so happy at your work." "Yes," said the other, "mine is a golden trade; a good grinder never puts his hand in his pocket without finding money in it – but where did you get that beautiful goose?" "I did not buy it, but changed a pig for it." "And where did you get the pig?" "I gave a cow for it." "And the cow?" "I gave a horse for it." "And the horse?" "I gave a piece of silver as big as my head for that." "And the silver?" "Oh! I worked hard for that seven long years." "You have thriven well in the world hitherto," said the grinder; "now if you could find money in your pocket whenever you put your hand into it, your fortune would be made." "Very true: but how is that to be managed?" "You must turn grinder like me," said the other; "you only want a grindstone; the rest will come of itself. Here is one that is a little the worse for wear: I would not ask more than the value of your goose for it – will you buy?" "How can you ask such a question?" replied Hans. "I should be the happiest man in the world, if I could have money whenever I put my hand in my pocket; what could I want more? There's the goose!" "Now," said the grinder, as he gave him a common rough stone that lay by his side, "this is a most capital stone; do but manage it cleverly, and you can make an old nail cut with it."

Hans took the stone and went off with a light

heart: his eyes sparkled for joy, and he said to himself, "I must have been born in a lucky hour; everything that I want or wish for comes to me of itself."

Meantime he began to be tired, for he had been travelling ever since daybreak; he was hungry too, for he had given away his last penny in his joy at getting the cow. At last he could go no farther, and the stone tired him terribly; he dragged himself to the side of a pond, that he might drink some water, and rest a while; so he laid the stone carefully by his side on the bank: but as he stooped down to drink, he forgot it, pushed it a little, and down it went plump into the pond. For a while he watched it sinking in the deep clear water, then sprang up for joy, and again fell upon his knees, and thanked heaven with tears in his eyes for its kindness in taking away his only plague, the ugly heavy stone. "How happy am I!" cried he. "No mortal was ever so lucky as I am." Then up he got with a light and merry heart and walked on free from all his troubles, till he reached his mother's house.

THE TRAVELLING MUSICIANS

AN honest farmer had once an ass, who had been a faithful servant to him a great many years, but was now growing old and every day more and more unfit for work. His master therefore was tired of keeping him and began to think of putting an end to him; but the ass, who saw that some mischief was in the wind, took himself slyly off, and began his journey towards the great city, "for there," thought he, "I may turn musician."

After he had travelled a little way, he spied a dog lying by the roadside and panting as if he were very tired. "What makes you pant so, my friend?" said the ass. "Alas!" said the dog, "my master was going to knock me on the head, because I am old and weak, and can no longer make myself useful to him in hunting; so I ran away: but what can I do to earn my livelihood?" "Hark ye!" said the ass, "I am going to the great city to turn musician: suppose you go with me, and try what you can do in the same way?" The dog said he was willing, and they jogged on together.

They had not gone far before they saw a cat sitting in the middle of the road and making a most rueful face. "Pray, my good lady," said the ass, "what's the matter with you? You look quite out of spirits!" "Ah me!" said the cat, "how can one be in good spirits when one's life is in danger? Because I am beginning to grow old, and had rather lie at my ease by the fire than run about the house after the mice, my mistress laid hold of me, and was going to drown me; and though I have been lucky enough to get away from her, I do not know what I am to live upon." "O!" said the ass, "by all means go with us to the great city; you are a good night singer, and may make your fortune as a musician." The cat was pleased with the thought, and joined the party.

Soon afterwards, as they were passing by a farmyard, they saw a cock perched upon a gate, and screaming out with all his might and main. "Bravo!" said the ass; "upon my word you make a famous noise; pray what is all this about?" "Why," said the cock, "I was just now saying that we should have fine weather for our washing-day, and yet my mistress and the cook don't thank me for my pains, but threaten to cut off my head tomorrow, and make broth of me for the guests that are coming on Sunday!" "Heaven forbid!" said the ass; "come with us, Master Chanticleer; it will be better, at any rate, than staying here to have your head cut off! Besides, who knows? If we take care to sing in tune, we may get up some kind of a concert: so come along with us." "With all my heart," said the cock: so they all four went on jollily together.

They could not, however, reach the great city the first day; so when night came on, they went into a wood to sleep. The ass and the dog laid themselves down under a great tree, and the cat climbed up into the branches; while the cock, thinking that the higher he sat the safer he should be, flew up to the very top of the tree, and then, according to his custom, before he went to sleep, looked out on all sides of him to see that everything

was well. In doing this, he saw far off something
bright and shining; and calling to his companions
said, "There must be a house no great way off, for
I see a light." "If that be the case," said the ass, "we
had better change our quarters, for our lodging is
not the best in the world!" "Besides," added the
dog, "I should not be the worse for a bone or two,
or a bit of meat." So they walked off together
towards the spot where Chanticleer had seen the
light; and as they drew near, it became larger and
brighter, till they at last came close to a house in
which a gang of robbers lived.

The ass, being the tallest of the company,
marched up to the window and peeped in. "Well,
Donkey," said Chanticleer, "what do you see?"
"What do I see?" replied the ass, "why I see a table
spread with all kinds of good things, and robbers
sitting round it making merry." "That would be a
noble lodging for us," said the cock. "Yes," said
the ass, "if we could only get in:" so they consulted
together how they should contrive to get the robbers out; and at last they hit upon a plan. The ass
placed himself upright on his hind legs, with his

forefeet resting against the window; the dog got upon his back; the cat scrambled up to the dog's shoulders, and the cock flew up and sat upon the cat's head. When all was ready, a signal was given, and they began their music. The ass brayed, the dog barked, the cat mewed, and the cock screamed; and then they all broke through the window at once, and came tumbling into the room, amongst the broken glass, with a most hideous clatter! The robbers, who had been not a little frightened by the opening concert, had now no doubt that some frightful hobgoblin had broken in upon them, and scampered away as fast as they could.

The coast once clear, our travellers soon sat down, and dispatched what the robbers had left, with as much eagerness as if they had not expected to eat again for a month. As soon as they had satisfied themselves, they put out the lights, and each once more sought out a resting-place to his own liking. The ass laid himself down upon a heap of straw in the yard; the dog stretched himself upon a mat behind the door; the cat rolled herself up on the hearth before the warm ashes; and the cock perched upon a beam on top of the house; and, as they were all rather tired with their journey, they soon fell asleep.

But about midnight, when the robbers saw from afar that the lights were out and that all seemed quiet, they began to think that they had been in too great a hurry to run away; and one of them, who was bolder than the rest, went to see what was going on. Finding everything still, he marched into the kitchen, and groped about till he found a match in order to light a candle; and then, espying the glittering fiery eyes of the cat, he mistook them for live coals, and held the match to them to light it. But the cat, not understanding this joke, sprung at his face, and spit, and scratched at him. This frightened him dreadfully, and away he ran to the back door; but there the dog jumped up and bit him in the leg; and as he was crossing over the yard the ass kicked him; and the cock, who had been awakened by the noise, crowed with all his might. At this the robber ran back as fast as he could to his comrades, and told the captain "how a horrid witch had got into the house, and had spit at him and scratched his face with her long bony fingers; how a man with a knife in his hand had hidden himself behind the door, and stabbed him in the leg; how a black monster stood in the yard and struck him with a club, and how the devil sat upon the top of the house and cried out, "Throw the rascal up here!" After this the robbers never dared to go back to the house: but the musicians were so pleased with their quarters, that they took up their abode there; and there they are, I dare say, at this very day.

THE GOLDEN BIRD

A CERTAIN king had a beautiful garden, and in the garden stood a tree which bore golden apples. These apples were always counted, and about the time when they began to grow ripe it was found that every night one of them was gone. The king became very angry at this, and ordered the gardener to keep watch all night under the tree. The gardener set his eldest son to watch; but about twelve o'clock he fell asleep, and in the morning another of the apples was missing. Then the second son was ordered to watch; and at midnight he too fell asleep, and in the morning another apple was gone. Then the third son offered to keep watch; but the gardener at first would not let him, for fear some harm should come to him: however, at last he consented, and the young man laid himself under the tree to watch. As the clock struck twelve he heard a rustling noise in the air, and a bird came flying that was of pure gold; and as it was snapping at one of the apples with its beak, the gardener's son jumped up and shot an arrow at it. But the arrow did the bird no harm; only it dropped a golden feather from its tail, and then flew away. The golden feather was brought to the king in the morning, and all the council was called together. Everyone agreed that it was worth more than all the wealth of the kingdom: but the king said, "One feather is of no use to me, I must have the whole bird."

Then the gardener's eldest son set out and thought to find the golden bird very easily; and when he had gone but a little way, he came to a wood, and by the side of the wood he saw a fox sitting; so he took his bow and made ready to shoot at it. Then the fox said, "Do not shoot me, for I will give you good counsel; I know what your business is, and that you want to find the golden bird. You will reach a village in the evening; and when you get there, you will see two inns opposite

to each other, one of which is very pleasant and
beautiful to look at: go not in there, but rest for the
night in the other, though it may appear to you to
be very poor and mean." But the son thought to
himself, "What can such a beast as this know about
the matter?" So he shot his arrow at the fox; but he
missed it, and it set up its tail above its back and
ran into the wood. Then he went his way, and in
the evening came to the village where the two inns
were; and in one of these were people singing, and
dancing, and feasting; but the other looked very
dirty, and poor. "I should be very silly," said he,
"if I went to that shabby house, and left this
charming place;" so he went into the smart house,
and ate and drank at his ease, and forgot the bird,
and his country too.

Time passed on; and as the eldest son did not
come back and no tidings were heard of him, the
second son set out, and the same thing happened to
him. He met the fox, who gave him the same good
advice: but when he came to the two inns, his eldest
brother was standing at the window where the
merrymaking was, and called to him to come in;
and he could not withstand the temptation, but

went in, and forgot the golden bird and his country in the same manner.

Time passed on again, and the youngest son too wished to set out into the wild world to seek for the golden bird; but his father would not listen to it for a long while, for he was very fond of his son, and was afraid that some ill luck might happen to him also, and prevent his coming back. However, at last it was agreed he should go, for he would not rest at home; and as he came to the wood, he met the fox, and heard the same good counsel. But he was thankful to the fox, and did not attempt his life as his brothers had done; so the fox said, "Sit upon my tail, and you will travel faster." So he sat down, and the fox began to run, and away they went over stock and stone so quick that their hair whistled in the wind.

When they came to the village, the son followed the fox's counsel, and without looking about him went to the shabby inn and rested there all night at his ease. In the morning came the fox again and met him as he was beginning his journey, and said, "Go straight forward, till you come to a castle, before which lie a whole troop of soldiers fast asleep and snoring: take no notice of them, but go into the castle and pass on and on till you come to a room, where the golden bird sits in a wooden cage; close by it stands a beautiful golden cage; but do not try to take the bird out of the shabby cage and put it into the handsome one, otherwise you will repent it." Then the fox stretched out his tail again, and the young man sat himself down, and away they went over stock and stone till their hair whistled in the wind.

Before the castle gate all was as the fox had said: so the son went in and found the chamber where the golden bird hung in a wooden cage, and below stood the golden cage, and the three golden apples that had been lost were lying close by it. Then thought he to himself, "It will be a very droll thing to bring away such a fine bird in this shabby cage;" so he opened the door and took hold of it and put it into the golden cage. But the bird set up such a loud scream that all the soldiers awoke, and they took him prisoner and carried him before the king. The next morning the court sat to judge him; and when all was heard, it sentenced him to die, unless he should bring the king the golden horse which could run as swiftly as the wind; and if he did this, he was to have the golden bird given him for his own.

So he set out once more on his journey, sighing, and in great despair, when on a sudden his good friend the fox met him, and said, "You see now what has happened on account of your not listening to my counsel. I will still, however, tell you how to find the golden horse, if you will do as I bid you. You must go straight on till you come to the castle where the horse stands in his stall: by his side will lie the groom fast asleep and snoring: take away the horse quietly, but be sure to put the old leathern saddle upon him, and not the golden one that is close by it." Then the son sat down on the fox's tail, and away they went over stock and stone till their hair whistled in the wind.

All went right, and the groom lay snoring with his hand upon the golden saddle. But when the son looked at the horse, he thought it a great pity to put the leathern saddle upon it. "I will give him the good one," said he; "I am sure he deserves it." As he took up the golden saddle the groom awoke and cried out so loud, that all the guards ran in and took him prisoner, and in the morning he was again brought before the court to be judged, and was sentenced to die. But it was agreed, that, if he could bring thither the beautiful princess, he should live, and have the bird and the horse given him for his own.

Then he went his way again very sorrowful; but the old fox came and said, "Why did not you listen to me? If you had, you would have carried away both the bird and the horse; yet will I once more give you counsel. Go straight on, and in the evening you will arrive at a castle. At twelve o'clock at night the princess goes to the bathing-house: go up to her and give her a kiss, and she will let you lead her away; but take care you do not suffer her to go and take leave of her father and mother." Then the fox stretched out his tail, and so away they went over stock and stone till their hair whistled again.

As they came to the castle, all was as the fox had said, and at twelve o'clock the young man met the princess going to the bath and gave her the kiss, and she agreed to run away with him, but begged with many tears that he would let her take leave of her father. At first he refused, but she wept still more and more, and fell at his feet, till at last he consented; but the moment she came to her father's house the guards awoke and he was taken prisoner again.

Then he was brought before the king, and the king said, "You shall never have my daughter unless in eight days you dig away the hill that stops the view from my window." Now this hill was so big that the whole world could not take it away: and when he had worked for seven days, and had done very little, the fox came and said, "Lie down and go to sleep; I will work for you." And in the morning he awoke and the hill was gone; so he went merrily to the king, and told him that now that it was removed he must give him the princess.

Then the king was obliged to keep his word, and away went the young man and the princess; and the fox came and said to him, "We will have all three, the princess, the horse, and the bird." "Ah!" said the young man, "that would be a great thing, but how can you contrive it?"

"If you will only listen," said the fox, "it can soon be done. When you come to the king, and he asks for the beautiful princess, you must say, 'Here she is!' Then he will be very joyful; and you will mount the golden horse that they are to give you, and put out your hand to take leave of them; but shake hands with the princess last. Then lift her quickly on to the horse behind you; clap your spurs to his side, and gallop away as fast as you can."

All went right: then the fox said, "When you come to the castle where the bird is, I will stay with the princess at the door, and you will ride in and speak to the king; and when he sees that it is the right horse, he will bring out the bird; but you must sit still, and say that you want to look at it, to see whether it is the true golden bird; and when you get it into your hand, ride away."

This, too, happened as the fox said; they carried off the bird, the princess mounted again, and they rode on to a great wood. Then the fox came, and said, "Pray kill me, and cut off my head and my feet." But the young man refused to do it: so the fox said, "I will at any rate give you good counsel: beware of two things; ransom no one from the gallows, and sit down by the side of no river."

Then away he went. "Well," thought the young man, "it is no hard matter to keep that advice."

He rode on with the princess, till at last he came to the village where he had left his two brothers. And there he heard a great noise and uproar; and when he asked what was the matter, the people said, "Two men are going to be hanged." As he came nearer, he saw that the two men were his brothers, who had turned robbers; so he said, "Cannot they in any way be saved?" But the people said "No," unless he would bestow all his money upon the rascals and buy their liberty. Then he did not stay to think about the matter, but paid what was asked, and his brothers were given up, and went on with him towards their home.

And as they came to the wood where the fox first met them, it was so cool and pleasant that the two brothers said, "Let us sit down by the side of the river, and rest a while, to eat and drink." So he said, "Yes," and forgot the fox's counsel, and sat down on the side of the river; and while he suspected nothing, they came behind, and threw him down the bank, and took the princess, the horse, and the bird, and went home to the king their master, and said, "All this have we won by our labour." Then there was great rejoicing made; but the horse would not eat, the bird would not sing, and the princess wept.

The youngest son fell to the bottom of the river's bed: luckily it was nearly dry, but his bones were almost broken, and the bank was so steep that he could find no way to get out. Then the old fox came once more, and scolded him for not following his advice; otherwise no evil would have befallen him: "Yet," said he, "I cannot leave you here, so lay hold of my tail and hold fast." Then he pulled him out of the river, and said to him, as he got upon the bank, "Your brothers have set watch to kill you, if they find you in the kingdom." So he dressed himself as a poor man, and came secretly to the king's court, and was scarcely within the doors when the horse began to eat, and the bird to sing, and the princess left off weeping. Then he went to the king, and told him all his brothers' roguery; and they were seized and punished, and he had the princess given to him again; and after the king's death he was heir to his kingdom.

A long while after, he went to walk one day in the wood, and the old fox met him, and besought him with tears in his eyes to kill him, and cut off his head and feet. And at last he did so, and in a moment the fox was changed into a man, and turned out to be the brother of the princess, who had been lost a great many many years.

THE FISHERMAN AND HIS WIFE

THERE was once a fisherman who lived with his wife in a ditch, close by the seaside. The fisherman used to go out all day a-fishing; and one day, as he sat on the shore with his rod, looking at the shining water and watching his line, all on a sudden his float was dragged away deep under the sea: and in drawing it up he pulled a great fish out of the water. The fish said to him, "Pray let me live: I am not a real fish; I am an enchanted prince, put me in the water again, and let me go." "Oh!" said the man, "you need not make so many words about the matter; I wish to have nothng to do with a fish that can talk; so swim away as soon as you please." Then he put him back into the water, and the fish darted straight down to the bottom, and left a long streak of blood behind him.

When the fisherman went home to his wife in the ditch, he told her how he had caught a great fish, and how it had told him it was an enchanted prince, and that on hearing it speak he had let it go again. "Did you not ask it for anything?" said the wife. "No," said the man, "what should I ask for?" "Ah!" said the wife, "we live very wretchedly here in this nasty stinking ditch; do go back, and tell the fish we want a little cottage."

The fisherman did not much like the business: however, he went to the sea, and when he came there the water looked all yellow and green. And he stood at the water's edge, and said,

> "O man of the sea!
> Come listen to me,
> For Alice my wife,
> The plague of my life,
> Hath sent me to beg a boon of thee!"

Then the fish came swimming to him, and said, "Well, what does she want?" "Ah!" answered the fisherman, "my wife says that when I had caught you, I ought to have asked you for something before I let you go again; she does not like living any longer in the ditch, and wants a little cottage." "Go home, then," said the fish, "she is in the cottage already." So the man went home, and saw his wife standing at the door of a cottage. "Come in, come in," said she; "is not this much better than the ditch?" And there was a parlour, and a bed-chamber, and a kitchen; and behind the cottage there was a little garden with all sorts of flowers and fruits, and a courtyard full of ducks and chickens. "Ah!" said the fisherman, "how happily we shall live!" "We will try to do so at least," said his wife.

Everything went right for a week or two, and then Dame Alice said, "Husband, there is not room enough in this cottage, the courtyard and garden are a great deal too small; I should like to have a large stone castle to live in; so go to the fish again, and tell him to give us a castle." "Wife," said the fisherman, "I don't like to go to him again, for perhaps he will be angry; we ought to be content with the cottage." "Nonsense!" said the wife. "He will do it very willingly; go along, and try."

The fisherman went; but his heart was very

heavy: and when he came to the sea, it looked blue and gloomy, though it was quite calm, and he went close to it, and said,

> "O man of the sea!
> Come listen to me,
> For Alice my wife
> The plague of my life,
> Hath sent me to beg a boon of thee!"

"Well, what does she want now?" said the fish. "Ah!" said the man very sorrowfully, "my wife wants to live in a stone castle." "Go home then," said the fish, "she is standing at the door of it already." So away went the fisherman, and found his wife standing before a great castle. "See," said she, "is not this grand?" With that they went into the castle together, and found a great many servants there, and the rooms all richly furnished and full of golden chairs and tables; and behind the castle was a garden, and a wood half a mile long, full of sheep, and goats, and hares, and deer; and in the courtyard were stables and cow-houses. "Well," said the man, "now will we live contented and happy in this beautiful castle for the rest of our lives." "Perhaps we may," said the wife; "but let us consider and sleep upon it before we make up our minds:" so they went to bed.

The next morning, when Dame Alice awoke, it was broad daylight, and she jogged the fisherman with her elbow, and said, "Get up, husband, and bestir yourself, for we must be king of all the land." "Wife, wife," said the man, "why should we wish to be king? I will not be king." "Then I will," said Alice. "But, wife," answered the fisherman, "how can you be king? the fish cannot make you a king." "Husband," said she, "say no more about it, but go and try; I will be king!" So the man went away, quite sorrowful to think that his wife should want to be king. The sea looked a dark grey colour, and was covered with foam as he cried out,

> "O man of the sea!
> Come listen to me,
> For Alice my wife,
> The plague of my life,
> Hath sent me to beg a boon of thee!"

"Well, what would she have now?" said the fish. "Alas!" said the man, "my wife wants to be king." "Go home," said the fish; "she is king already."

Then the fisherman went home; and as he came close to the palace, he saw a troop of soldiers, and heard the sound of drums and trumpets; and when he entered in, he saw his wife sitting on a high throne of gold and diamonds, with a golden crown upon her head; and on each side of her stood six beautiful maidens, each a head taller than the other. "Well, wife," said the fisherman, "are you king?" "Yes," said she, "I am king." And when he had looked at her for a long time, he said, "Ah, wife! what a fine thing it is to be king! Now we shall never have anything more to wish for." "I don't know how that may be," said she; "never is a long time. I am king, 'tis true, but I begin to be tired of it, and I think I should like to be emperor." "Alas, wife! Why should you wish to be emperor?" said the fisherman. "Husband," said she, "go to the fish; I say I will be emperor." "Ah, wife!" replied the fisherman. "The fish cannot make an emperor, and I should not like to ask for such a thing." "I am king," said Alice, "and you are my slave, so go directly!" So the fisherman was obliged to go; and he muttered as he went along. "This will come to no good, it is too much to ask, the fish will be tired at last, and then we shall repent of what we have done." He soon arrived at the sea, and the water was quite black and muddy, and a mighty whirlwind blew over it; but he went to the shore, and said,

> "O man of the sea!
> Come listen to me,
> For Alice my wife,
> The plague of my life,
> Hath sent me to beg a boon of thee!"

"What would she have now?" said the fish. "Ah!" said the fisherman. "She wants to be emperor." "Go home," said the fish; "she is emperor already."

So he went home again; and as he came near he saw his wife sitting on a very lofty throne made of solid gold, with a great crown on her head full two yards high, and on each side of her stood her guards and attendants in a row, each one smaller than the other, from the tallest giant down to a little dwarf no bigger than my finger. And before her stood princes, and dukes, and earls: and the fisherman went up to her and said, "Wife, are you emperor?" "Yes," said she, "I am emperor." "Ah!" said the man as he gazed

upon her, "what a fine thing it is to be emperor!"
"Husband," said she, "why should we stay at being
emperor; I will be pope next." "O wife, wife!" said
he. "How can you be pope? There is but one pope at
a time in Christendom." "Husband," said she, "I
will be pope this very day." "But," replied the
husband, "the fish cannot make you pope." "What
nonsense!" said she. "If he can make an emperor, he
can make a pope, go and try him." So the fisherman
went. But when he came to the shore the wind was
raging, and the sea was tossed up and down like
boiling water, and the ships were in the greatest
distress and danced upon the waves most fearfully;
in the middle of the sky there was a little blue, but
towards the south it was all red as if a dreadful storm
was rising. At this the fisherman was terribly
frightened, and trembled, so that his knees knocked
together: but he went to the shore and said,

> "O man of the sea!
> Come listen to me,
> For Alice my wife,
> The plague of my life,
> Hath sent me to beg a boon of thee!"

"What does she want now?" said the fish. "Ah!" said the fisherman. "My wife wants to be pope." "Go home," said the fish, "she is pope already."

Then the fisherman went home, and found his wife sitting on a throne that was two miles high; and she had three great crowns on her head, and around stood all the pomp and power of the Church; and on each side were two rows of burning lights, of all sizes, the greatest as large as the highest and biggest tower in the world, and the least no larger than a small rushlight. "Wife," said the fisherman as he looked at all this grandeur, "are you pope?" "Yes," said she, "I am pope." "Well, wife," replied he, "it is a grand thing to be pope; and now you must be content, for you can be nothing greater." "I will consider of that," said the wife. Then they went to bed: but Dame Alice could not sleep all night for thinking what she should be next. At last morning came, and the sun rose. "Ha!" thought she as she looked at it through the window. "Cannot I prevent the sun rising?" At this she was very angry, and she wakened her husband, and said, "Husband, go to the fish and tell him I want to be lord of the sun and moon." The

. . . and the heavens became black

fisherman was half asleep, but the thought frightened him so much, that he started and fell out of
bed. "Alas, wife!" said he. "Cannot you be content
to be pope?" "No," said she, "I am very uneasy,
and cannot bear to see the sun and moon rise
without my leave. Go to the fish directly."

Then the man went trembling for fear; and as
he was going down to the shore a dreadful storm
arose, so that the trees and the rocks shook; and the
heavens became black, and the lightning played,
and the thunder rolled; and you might have seen in
the sea great black waves like mountains with a
white crown of foam upon them; and the fisherman
said,

> "O man of the sea!
> Come listen to me,
> For Alice my wife,
> The plague of my life,
> Hath sent me to beg a boon of thee!"

"What does she want now?" said the fish.
"Ah!" said he, "she wants to be lord of the sun and
moon." "Go home," said the fish, "to your ditch
again!" And there they live to this very day.

THE TWELVE DANCING PRINCESSES

THERE was a king who had twelve beautiful daughters. They slept in twelve beds all in one room; and when they went to bed, the doors were shut and locked up; but every morning their shoes were found to be quite worn through as if they had been danced in all night; and yet nobody could find out how it happened, or where they had been.

Then the king made it known to all the land, that if any person could discover the secret, and find out where it was that the princesses danced in the night, he should have the one he liked best for his wife, and should be king after his death; but whoever tried and did not succeed, after three days and nights, should be put to death.

A king's son soon came. He was well entertained, and in the evening was taken to the chamber next to the one where the princesses lay in their twelve beds. There he was to sit and watch where they went to dance; and, in order that nothing might pass without his hearing it, the door of his chamber was left open. But the king's son soon fell asleep; and when he awoke in the morning he found that the princesses had all been dancing, for the soles of their shoes were full of holes. The same thing happened the second and third night: so the king ordered his head to be cut off. After him came several others; but they had all the same luck, and all lost their lives in the same manner.

Now it chanced that an old soldier, who had been wounded in battle and could fight no longer, passed through the country where this king reigned: and as he was travelling through a wood, he met an old woman, who asked him where he was going. "I hardly know where I am going, or what I had better do," said the soldier; "but I think I should like very well to find out where it is that the princesses dance, and then in time I might be a king." "Well," said the old dame, "that is no very hard task: only take care not to drink any of the wine which one of the princesses will bring to you in the evening; and as soon as she leaves you pretend to be fast asleep."

Then she gave him a cloak, and said, "As soon as you put that on you will become invisible, and you will then be able to follow the princesses wherever they go." When the soldier heard all this good counsel, he determined to try his luck: so he went to the king, and said he was willing to undertake the task.

He was as well received as the others had been, and the king ordered fine royal robes to be given him; and when the evening came he was led to the outer chamber. Just as he was going to lie down, the eldest of the princesses brought him a cup of wine; but the soldier threw it all away secretly, taking care not to drink a drop. Then he laid himself down on his bed, and in a little while began to snore very loud as if he was fast asleep. When the twelve princesses heard this they laughed heartily; and the eldest said, "This fellow too might have done a wiser thing than lose his life in this way!" Then they rose up and opened their drawers and

boxes, and took out all their fine clothes, and
dressed themselves at the glass, and skipped about
as if they were eager to begin dancing. But the
youngest said, "I don't know how it is, while you
are so happy I feel very uneasy; I am sure some
mischance will befall us." "You simpleton," said
the eldest, "you are always afraid; have you forgotten how many kings' sons have already watched us
in vain? And as for this soldier, even if I had not
given him his sleeping draught, he would have slept
soundly enough."

When they were all ready, they went and
looked at the soldier; but he snored on, and did not
stir hand or foot: so they thought they were quite
safe; and the eldest went up to her own bed and
clapped her hands, and the bed sunk into the floor
and a trap door flew open. The soldier saw them
going down through the trap door one after
another, the eldest leading the way; and thinking
he had no time to lose, he jumped up, put on the
cloak which the old woman had given him, and
followed them; but in the middle of the stairs he
trod on the gown of the youngest princess, and she
cried out to her sisters, "All is not right; someone

took hold of my gown." "You silly creature!" said the eldest. "It is nothing but a nail in the wall." Then down they all went, and at the bottom they found themselves in a most delightful grove of trees; and the leaves were all of silver, and glittered and sparkled beautifully. The soldier wished to take away some token of the place; so he broke off a little branch, and there came a loud noise from the tree. Then the youngest daughter said again, "I am sure all is not right – did not you hear that noise? That never happened before." But the eldest said, "It is only our princes, who are shouting for joy at our approach."

Then they came to another grove of trees, where all the leaves were of gold; and afterwards to a third, where the leaves were all glittering diamonds. And the soldier broke a branch from each; and every time there was a loud noise, which made the youngest sister tremble with fear; but the eldest still said, it was only the princes, who were crying for joy. So they went on till they came to a great lake; and at the side of the lake there lay twelve little boats with twelve handsome princes in them, who seemed to be waiting there for the princesses.

One of the princesses went into each boat, and the soldier stepped into the same boat with the youngest. As they were rowing over the lake, the prince who was in the boat with the youngest princess and the soldier said, "I do not know why it is, but though I am rowing with all my might we do not get on so fast as usual, and I am quite tired: the boat seems very heavy today." "It is only the heat of the weather," said the princess; "I feel it very warm too."

On the other side of the lake stood a fine illuminated castle, from which came the merry music of horns and trumpets. There they all landed, and went into the castle, and each prince danced with his princess; and the soldier, who was all the time invisible, danced with them too; and when any of the princesses had a cup of wine set by her, he drank it all up, so that when she put the cup to her mouth it was empty. At this, too, the youngest sister was terribly frightened, but the eldest always silenced her. They danced on till three o'clock in the morning, and then all their shoes were worn out, so that they were obliged to leave off. The princes rowed them back again over the lake; (but this time the soldier placed himself in the boat with the eldest princess;) and on the opposite shore they took leave of each other, the princesses promising to come again the next night.

When they came to the stairs, the soldier ran on before the princesses, and laid himself down; and as the twelve sisters slowly came up very much tired, they heard him snoring in his bed; so they said, "Now all is quite safe;" then they undressed themselves, put away their fine clothes, pulled off their shoes, and went to bed. In the morning the soldier said nothing about what had happened, but determined to see more of this strange adventure, and went again the second and third night; and everything happened just as before; the princesses danced each time till their shoes were worn to pieces, and then returned home. However, on the third night the soldier carried away one of the golden cups as a token of where he had been.

As soon as the time came when he was to declare the secret, he was taken before the king with the three branches and the golden cup; and the twelve princesses stood listening behind the door to hear what he would say. And when the king asked him, "Where do my twelve daughters dance at night?" he answered, "With twelve princes in a castle underground." And then he told the king all that had happened, and showed him the three branches and the golden cup which he had brought with him. Then the king called for the princesses, and asked them whether what the soldier said was true: and when they saw that they were discovered, and that it was of no use to deny what had happened, they confessed it all. And the king asked the soldier which of them he would choose for his wife; and he answered, "I am not very young, so I will have the eldest." – And they were married that very day, and the soldier was chosen to be the king's heir.

ROSE-BUD

ONCE upon a time there lived a king and queen who had no children; and this they lamented very much. But one day as the queen was walking by the side of the river, a little fish lifted its head out of the water, and said, "Your wish shall be fulfilled, and you shall soon have a daughter." What the little fish had foretold soon came to pass; and the queen had a little girl who was so very beautiful that the king could not cease looking on her for joy, and determined to hold a great feast. So he invited not only his relations, friends, and neighbours, but also all the fairies, that they might be kind and good to his little daughter.

Now there were thirteen fairies in his kingdom,

and he had only twelve golden dishes for them to eat out of, so that he was obliged to leave one of the fairies without an invitation. The rest came, and after the feast was over they gave all their best gifts to the little princess: one gave her virtue, another beauty, another riches, and so on till she had all that was excellent in the world. When eleven had done blessing her, the thirteenth, who had not been invited, and was very angry on that account, came in, and determined to take her revenge. So she cried out, "The king's daughter shall in her fifteenth year be wounded by a spindle, and fall down dead."

Then the twelfth, who had not yet given her gift, came forward and said that the bad wish must be fulfilled, but that she could soften it, and that the king's daughter should not die, but fall asleep for a hundred years.

But the king hoped to save his dear child from the threatened evil, and ordered that all the spindles in the kingdom should be bought up and destroyed. All the fairies' gifts were in the meantime fulfilled; for the princess was so beautiful, and well-behaved, and amiable, and wise, that everyone who knew her loved her. Now it happened that on the very day she was fifteen years old the king and queen were not at home, and she was left alone in the palace. So she roved about by herself, and looked at all the rooms and chambers, till at last she came to an old tower, to which there was a narrow staircase ending with a little door. In the door there was a golden key, and when she turned it the door sprang open, and there sat an old lady spinning away very busily.

"Why, how now, good mother," said the princess, "what are you doing there?" "Spinning," said the old lady, and nodded her head. "How prettily that little thing turns round!" said the princess, and took the spindle and began to spin. But scarcely had she touched it, before the prophecy was fulfilled, and she fell down lifeless on the ground.

However, she was not dead, but had only fallen into a deep sleep; and the king and the queen, who just then came home, and all their court, fell asleep too; and the horses slept in the stables, and the dogs in the courtyard, the pigeons on the house-top and the flies on the walls. Even the fire on the hearth left off blazing, and went to sleep; and the meat that was roasting stood still; and the cook, who was at that moment pulling the kitchen-boy by the hair to give him a box on the ear for something he had done amiss, let him go, and both fell asleep; and so everything stood still, and slept soundly.

A large hedge of thorns soon grew round the palace, and every year it became higher and thicker, till at last the whole palace was surrounded and hid, so that not even the roof or the chimneys could be seen. But there went a report through all the land of the beautiful sleeping Rose-Bud (for so was the king's daughter called); so that from time to time several kings' sons came, and tried to break through the thicket into the palace. This they could never do; for the thorns and bushes laid hold of them as it were with hands, and there they stuck fast and died miserably.

After many many years there came a king's son into that land, and an old man told him the story of the thicket of thorns, and how a beautiful palace stood behind it, in which was a wondrous princess, called Rose-Bud, asleep with all her court. He told, too, how he had heard from his grandfather that many many princes had come, and had tried to break through the thicket, but had stuck fast and died. Then the young prince said, "All this shall not frighten me, I will go and see Rose-Bud." The old man tried to dissuade him, but he persisted in going.

Now that very day were the hundred years completed; and as the prince came to the thicket, he saw nothing but beautiful flowering shrubs, through which he passed with ease, and they closed after him as firm as ever. Then he came at last to the palace, and there in the courtyard lay the dogs asleep, and the horses in the stables, and on the roof sat the pigeons fast asleep with their heads under their wings; and when he came into the palace, the flies slept on the walls, and the cook in the kitchen was still holding up her hand as if she would beat the boy, and the maid sat with a black fowl in her hand ready to be plucked.

Then he went on still farther, and all was so still that he could hear every breath he drew; till at last he came to the old tower and opened the door of the little room in which Rose-Bud was, and there she lay fast asleep, and looked so beautiful that he could not take his eyes off her, and he stooped down and gave her a kiss. But the

moment he kissed her she opened her eyes and
awoke, and smiled upon him. Then they went out
together, and presently the king and queen also
awoke, and all the court, and they gazed on each
other with great wonder. And the horses got up
and shook themselves, and the dogs jumped about
and barked; the pigeons took their heads from
under their wings, and looked about and flew into
the fields; the flies on the walls buzzed away; the
fire in the kitchen blazed up and cooked the dinner,
and the roast meat turned round again; the cook
gave the boy the box on his ear so that he cried
out, and the maid went on plucking the fowl. And
then was the wedding of the prince and Rose-Bud
celebrated, and they lived happily together all their
lives long.

TOM THUMB

THERE was once a poor woodman sitting by the fire in his cottage, and his wife sat by his side spinning. "How lonely it is," said he, "for you and me to sit here by ourselves without any children to play about and amuse us, while other people seem so happy and merry with their children!" "What you say is very true," said the wife, sighing and turning round her wheel, "how happy should I be if I had but one child! And if it were ever so small, nay, if it were no bigger than my thumb, I should be very happy, and love it dearly." Now it came to pass that this good woman's wish was fulfilled just as she desired; for, some time afterwards, she had a little boy who was quite healthy and strong, but not much bigger than my thumb. So they said, "Well, we cannot say we have not got what we wished for, and, little as he is, we all love him dearly;" and they called him Tom Thumb.

They gave him plenty of food, yet he never grew bigger, but remained just the same size as when he was born; still his eyes were sharp and sparkling, and he soon showed himself to be a clever little fellow, who always knew well what he was about. One day, as the woodman was getting ready to go into the wood to cut fuel, he said, "I wish I had someone to bring the cart after me, for I want to make haste." "O Father!" cried Tom. "I will take care of that; the cart shall be in the wood by the time you want it." Then the woodman laughed, and said, "How can that be? You cannot reach up to the horse's bridle." "Never mind that, Father," said Tom; "if my mother will only harness the horse, I will get into his ear and tell him which way to go." "Well," said the father, "we will try for once."

When the time came, the mother harnessed the horse to the cart, and put Tom into his ear; and as he sat there, the little man told the beast how to go, crying out, "Go on," and "Stop," as he wanted; so the horse went on just as if the woodman had driven it himself into the wood. It happened that, as the horse was going a little too fast, and Tom was calling out "Gently! gently!" two strangers came up. "What an odd thing that is!" said one. "There is a cart going along and I hear a carter talking to the horse, but can see no one." "That is strange," said the other; "let us follow the cart and see where it goes." So they went on into the wood, till at last they came to the place where the woodman was. Then Tom Thumb, seeing his father, cried out, "See, Father, here I am, with the cart, all right and safe; now take me down." So his father took hold of the horse with one hand, and with the other took his son out of the ear; then he put him down upon a straw, where he sat as merry as you please. The two strangers were all this time looking on, and did not know what to say for wonder. At last one took the other aside and said, "That little urchin will make our fortune if we can get him and carry him about from town to town as a show: we must buy him." So they went to the woodman and asked him what he would take for the little man: "He will be better off," said they, "with us than with you." "I won't sell him at all," said the father, "my own flesh and blood is dearer to me than all the silver and gold in the world." But Tom, hearing of the bargain they wanted to make, crept up his father's coat to his shoulder, and whispered in his ear, "Take the money, Father, and let them have me, I'll soon come back to you."

So the woodman at last agreed to sell Tom to the strangers for a large piece of gold. "Where do you like to sit?" said one of them. "Oh! put me on the rim of your hat, that will be a nice gallery for me; I can walk about there, and see the country as we go along." So they did as he wished; and when Tom had taken leave of his father, they took him away with them. They journeyed on till it began to be dusky, and then the little man said, "Let me get down, I'm tired." So the man took off his hat and set him down on a clod of earth in a ploughed field by the side of the road. But Tom ran about amongst the furrows, and at last slipped into an old mouse-hole. "Good night, masters," said he, "I'm off! Mind and look sharp after me the next time." They ran directly to the place, and poked the ends of their sticks into the mouse-hole, but all in vain;

they poked their sticks into the mouse-hole

Tom only crawled farther and farther in, and at last it became quite dark, so that they were obliged to go their way without their prize, as sulky as you please.

When Tom found they were gone, he came out of his hiding place. "What dangerous walking it is," said he, "in this ploughed field! If I were to fall from one of these great clods, I should certainly break my neck." At last, by good luck, he found a large empty snail shell. "This is lucky," said he. "I can sleep here very well," and in he crept. Just as he was falling asleep he heard two men passing, and one said to the other, "How shall we manage to steal that rich parson's silver and gold?" "I'll tell you," cried Tom. "What noise was that?" said the thief, frightened. "I am sure I heard someone speak." They stood still listening, and Tom said, "Take me with you, and I'll soon show you how to get the parson's money." "But where are you?" said they. "Look about on the ground," answered he, "and listen where the sound comes from." At last the thieves found him out, and lifted him up in their hands. "You little urchin!" said they. "What can you do for us?" "Why I can get between the iron window-bars of the parson's house, and throw you out whatever you want." "That's a good thought," said the thieves. "Come along, we shall see what you can do."

When they came to the parson's house, Tom slipped through the window-bars into the room, and then called out as loud as he could bawl, "Will you have all that is here?" At this the thieves were frightened, and said, "Softly, softly! Speak low, that you may not awaken anybody." But Tom pretended not to understand them, and bawled out again, "How much will you have? Shall I throw it all out?" Now the cook lay in the next room, and hearing a noise she raised herself in her bed and listened. Meantime the thieves were frightened, and ran off to a little distance; but at last they plucked up courage, and said, "The little urchin is only trying to make fools of us." So they came back and whispered softly to him, saying, "Now let us have no more of your jokes, but throw out some of the money." Then Tom called out as loud as he could, "Very well: hold your hands, here it comes." The cook heard this quite plain, so she sprang out of bed and ran to open the door. The thieves ran off as if a wolf was at their tails; and the maid, having groped about and found nothing, went away for a light. By the time she returned, Tom had slipped off into the barn; and when the cook had looked about and searched every hole and corner, and found nobody, she went to bed, thinking she must have been dreaming with her eyes open. The little man crawled about in the hayloft, and at last found a glorious place to finish his night's rest in; so he laid himself down, meaning to sleep till daylight, and then find his way home to his father and mother. But, alas! How cruelly was he disappointed! What

crosses and sorrows happen in this world! The cook
got up early before daybreak to feed the cows: she
went straight to the hayloft, and carried away a
large bundle of hay with the little man in the middle
of it fast asleep. He still, however, slept on, and did
not awake till he found himself in the mouth of the
cow, who had taken him up with a mouthful of
hay. "Good lack-a-day!" said he. "How did I
manage to tumble into the mill?" But he soon found
out where he really was, and was obliged to have
all his wits about him in order that he might not get
between the cow's teeth, and so be crushed to
death. At last down he went into her stomach. "It
is rather dark here," said he; "they forgot to build
windows in this room to let the sun in: a candle
would be no bad thing."

Though he made the best of his bad luck, he
did not like his quarters at all; and the worst of it
was, that more and more hay was always coming
down, and the space in which he was became
smaller and smaller. At last he cried out as loud as
he could, "Don't bring me any more hay! Don't
bring me any more hay!" The maid happened to be
just then milking the cow, and hearing someone

speak and seeing nobody, and yet being quite sure it was the same voice that she had heard in the night, she was so frightened that she fell off her stool and overset the milk pail. She ran off as fast as she could to her master the parson, and said, "Sir, sir, the cow is talking!" But the parson said, "Woman, thou art surely mad!" However, he went with her into the cow-house to see what was the matter. Scarcely had they set their foot on the threshold, when Tom called out, "Don't bring me any more hay!" Then the parson himself was frightened; and thinking the cow was surely bewitched, ordered that she should be killed directly. So the cow was killed, and the stomach, in which Tom lay, was thrown out upon a dunghill.

Tom soon set himself to work to get out, which was not a very easy task; but at last, just as he had made room to get his head out, a new misfortune befell him: a hungry wolf sprang out, and swallowed the whole stomach with Tom in it at a single gulp, and ran away. Tom, however, was not disheartened; and, thinking the wolf would not dislike having some chat with him as he was going along, he called out, "My good friend, I can show you a famous treat." "Where's that?" said the wolf. "In such and such a house," said Tom, describing his father's house, "you can crawl through the drain into the kitchen, and there you will find cakes, ham, beef, and everything your heart can desire." The wolf did not want to be asked twice; so that very night he went to the house and crawled through the drain into the kitchen, and ate and drank there to his heart's content. As soon as he was satisfied, he wanted to get away, but he had eaten so much that he could not get out the same way that he came in. This was just what Tom had reckoned upon; and he now began to set up a great shout, making all the noise he could. "Will you be quiet?" said the wolf. "You'll awaken everybody in the house." "What's that to me?" said the little man. "You have had your frolic, now I've a mind to be merry myself;" and he began again singing and shouting as loud as he could.

The woodman and his wife, being awakened by the noise, peeped through a crack in the door; but when they saw that the wolf was there, you may well suppose that they were terribly frightened; and the woodman ran for his axe, and gave his wife a scythe. – "Now do you stay behind," said the woodman; "and when I have knocked him on the head, do you rip up his belly for him with the scythe." Tom heard all this, and said, "Father, father! I am here, the wolf has swallowed me:" and his father said, "Heaven be praised! We have found our dear child again;" and he told his wife not to use the scythe, for fear she should hurt him. Then he aimed a great blow, and struck the wolf on the head, and killed him on the spot; and when he was dead they cut open his body and set Tommy free. "Ah!" said the father. "What fears we have had for you!" "Yes, Father," answered he, "I have travelled all over the world, since we parted, in one way or other; and now I am very glad to get fresh air again." "Why, where have you been?" said his father. "I have been in a mouse-hole, in a snail-shell, down a cow's throat, and in the wolf's belly; and yet here I am again safe and sound." "Well," said they, "we will not sell you again for all the riches in the world." So they hugged and kissed their dear little son, and gave him plenty to eat and drink, and fetched new clothes for him, for his old ones were quite spoiled on his journey.

THE GRATEFUL BEASTS

A CERTAIN man, who had lost almost all his money, resolved to set off with the little that was left him, and travel into the wide world. Then the first place he came to was a village, where the young people were running about crying and shouting. "What is the matter?" asked he. "See here," answered they, "we have got a mouse that we make dance to please us. Do look at him: what a droll sight it is! How he jumps about!" But the man pitied the poor little thing, and said, "Let the mouse go, and I will give you money." So he gave them some, and took the mouse and let him run; and he soon jumped into a hole that was close by, and was out of their reach.

Then he travelled on and came to another village, and there the children had got an ass that they made stand on its hind legs and tumble, at which they laughed and shouted, and gave the poor beast no rest. So the good man gave them also some money to let the poor ass alone.

At the next village he came to, the young people had got a bear that had been taught to dance, and they were plaguing the poor thing sadly. Then he gave them too some money to let the beast go, and the bear was very glad to get on his four feet, and seemed quite happy.

But the man had now given away all the money he had in the world, and had not a shilling in his pocket. Then said he to himself, "The king has heaps of gold in his treasury that he never uses; I cannot die of hunger, I hope I shall be forgiven if I borrow a little, and when I get rich again I will repay it all."

Then he managed to get into the treasury, and took a very little money; but as he came out the king's guards saw him; so they said he was a thief, and took him to the Judge, and he was sentenced to be thrown into the water in a box. The lid of the

box was full of holes to let in air, and a jug of water
and a loaf of bread were given him.

Whilst he was swimming along in the water
very sorrowfully, he heard something nibbling and
biting at the lock; and all of a sudden it fell off, the
lid flew open, and there stood his old friend the
little mouse, who had done him this service. And
then came the ass and the bear, and pulled the box
ashore; and all helped him because he had been kind
to them.

But now they did not know what to do next,
and began to consult together; when on a sudden a
wave threw on the shore a beautiful white stone
that looked like an egg. Then the bear said, "That's
a lucky thing: this is the wonderful stone, and
whoever has it may have everything else that he
wishes." So the man went and picked up the stone,
and wished for a palace and a garden, and a stud of
horses; and his wish was fulfilled as soon as he had
made it. And there he lived in his castle and garden,
with fine stables and horses; and all was so grand
and beautiful, that he never could wonder and gaze
at it enough.

After some time, some merchants passed by

that way. "See," said they, "what a princely palace! The last time we were here, it was nothing but a desert waste." They were ·very curious to know how all this had happened; so they went in and asked the master of the palace how it had been so quickly raised. "I have done nothing myself," answered he, "it is the wonderful stone that did all." "What a strange stone that must be!" said they: then he invited them in and showed it to them. They asked him whether he would sell it, and offered him all their goods for it; and the goods seemed so fine and costly, that he quite forgot that the stone would bring him in a moment a thousand better and richer things, and he agreed to make the bargain.

Scarcely was the stone, however, out of his hands before all his riches were gone, and he found himself sitting in his box in the water, with his jug of water and loaf of bread by his side. The grateful beasts, the mouse, the ass, and the bear, came directly to help him; but the mouse found she could not nibble off the lock this time, for it was a great deal stronger than before. Then the bear said, "We must find the wonderful stone again, or all our endeavours will be fruitless."

The merchants, meantime, had taken up their abode in the palace; so away went the three friends, and when they came near, the bear said, "Mouse, go in and look through the keyhole and see where the stone is kept: you are small, nobody will see you." The mouse did as she was told, but soon came back and said, "Bad news! I have looked in, and the stone hangs under the looking glass by a red silk string, and on each side of it sits a great cat with fiery eyes to watch it."

Then the others took counsel together and said, "Go back again, and wait till the master of the palace is in bed asleep, then nip his nose and pull his hair." Away went the mouse, and did as they directed her; and the master jumped up very angry, and rubbed his nose, and cried, "Those rascally cats are good for nothing at all, they let the mice eat my very nose and pull the hair off my head." Then he hunted them out of the room; and so the mouse had the best of the game.

Next night as soon as the master was asleep, the mouse crept in again, and nibbled at the red silk string to which the stone hung, till down it dropped, and she rolled it along to the door; but when it got there, the poor little mouse was quite tired; so she said to the ass, "Put in your foot, and lift it over the threshold." This was soon done: and they took up the stone, and set off for the waterside. Then the ass said, "How shall we reach the box?" But the bear answered, "That is easily managed; I can swim very well, and do you, donkey, put your forefeet over my shoulders; mind and hold fast, and take the stone in your mouth: as for you, mouse, you can sit in my ear."

It was all settled thus, and away they swam. After a time, the bear began to brag and boast. "We are brave fellows, are not we, ass?" said he. "What do you think?" But the ass held his tongue, and said not a word. "Why don't you answer me?" said the bear. "You must be an ill-mannered brute not to speak when you're spoken to." When the ass heard this, he could hold no longer; so he opened his mouth, and dropped the wonderful stone. "I could not speak," said he. "Did not you know I had the stone in my mouth? Now 'tis lost, and that's your fault." "Do but hold your tongue and be quiet," said the bear; "and let us think what's to be done."

Then a council was held: and at last they called

together all the frogs, their wives and families, relations and friends, and said: "A great enemy is coming to eat you all up; but never mind, bring us up plenty of stones, and we'll build a strong wall to guard you." The frogs hearing this were dreadfully frightened, and set to work, bringing up all the stones they could find. At last came a large fat frog pulling along the wonderful stone by the silken string: and when the bear saw it, he jumped for joy, and said, "Now we have found what we wanted." So he released the old frog from his load, and told him to tell his friends they might go about their business as soon as they pleased.

Then the three friends swam off again for the box; and the lid flew open, and they found that they were but just in time, for the bread was all eaten, and the jug almost empty. But as soon as the good man had the stone in his hand, he wished himself safe and sound in his palace again; and in a moment there he was, with his garden and his stables and his horses; and his three faithful friends dwelt with him, and they all spent their time happily and merrily as long as they lived.

JORINDA AND JORINDEL

THERE was once an old castle that stood in the middle of a large thick wood, and in the castle lived an old fairy. All the day long she flew about in the form of an owl, or crept about the country like a cat; but at night she always became an old woman again. When any youth came within a hundred paces of her castle, he became like stone, and could not move a step till she came and set him free: but when any pretty maiden came within that distance, she was changed into a bird; and the fairy put her into a cage and hung her up in a chamber in the castle. There were seven hundred of these cages hanging in the castle, and all with beautiful birds in them.

Now there was once a maiden whose name was Jorinda: she was prettier than all the pretty girls that ever were seen; and a shepherd whose name was Jorindel was her sweetheart; and they were soon to be married. One day they went to walk in the wood, that they might be alone: and Jorindel said, "We must take care that we don't go too near to the castle." It was a beautiful evening; the last rays of the setting sun shone bright through the high trees and touched the green underwood beneath while the turtledoves sang plaintively from the tall birches.

Jorinda sat down to gaze upon the sun; Jorindel sat by her side; and both felt sad, they knew not why; but it seemed as if they were to be parted from one another for ever. They had wandered far; and when they looked to see which way would lead to home, they found themselves at a loss to know what path to take.

The sun was setting fast, already half of its circle had disappeared behind the hill. Suddenly Jorindel looked behind him, and saw through the bushes that they had, without knowing it, come close under the old walls of the castle. He shrank

for fear, turned pale, and trembled. Jorinda was
singing,

> "The ring-dove sang from the willow spray,
>   Sorrow! Sorrow! Well-a-day!
> He mourn'd the fate
> Of his lovely mate,
>   Oh, sorrow, sorr – jugijugijug'

The song ceased suddenly. Jorindel turned to
see the reason, and beheld his Jorinda changed into
a nightingale; uttering only a mournful *jug, jug.* An
owl with fiery eyes flew three times round them,
and three times screamed *Tu whu! Tu whu! Tu
whu!* Jorindel could not move: he stood fixed as a
stone, and could neither weep, nor speak, nor stir
hand or foot. And now the sun went quite down;
the gloomy night came; the owl flew into a bush;
and a moment later the old fairy came forth, pale
and meagre, with staring eyes, and a nose and chin
that almost met one another.

She mumbled secret words, then seized the
nightingale, and went away with it in her hand.
Poor Jorindel saw that the nightingale was gone,
but what could he do? He could not move from the

spot where he stood. At last the fairy came back,
and sang with a hoarse voice,

> "Till the prisoner's fast,
> And her doom is cast,
>   There stay! Oh, stay!
> When the charm is around her,
> And the spell has bound her,
>   Hie away! Away!"

And at that moment Jorindel found himself
free. He fell on his knees before the fairy, and
prayed her to give him back his dear Jorinda: but
she said he should never see her again, and went
her way.

He prayed, he wept, he sorrowed, but all in
vain. "Alas!" he said. "What will become of me?"

He could not return to his own home, so he
went to a strange village, and employed himself in
keeping sheep. Many a time did he walk round and
round as near to the hated castle as he dared go. At
last he dreamed one night that he found a beautiful
purple flower, and in the middle of it lay a costly
pearl; and he dreamed that he plucked the flower,
and went with it in his hand into the castle, and

that everything he touched with it was freed from enchantment, and that there he found his dear Jorinda again.

In the morning when he awoke, he began to search over hill and dale for this pretty flower; and eight long days he sought for it in vain: but on the ninth day early in the morning he found the beautiful purple flower; and in the middle of it was a large dew drop as big as a costly pearl.

Then he plucked the flower, and set out and travelled day and night till he came again to the castle. Now he was less than a hundred paces away, and yet he did not turn into stone as before, but found that he could go close up to the door.

Jorindel was very glad to see this: he touched the door with the flower, and it sprang open. As he went within, he heard the voices of hundreds of singing birds. He followed the sound and came at last to a room where the fairy sat, with the seven hundred birds singing in the seven hundred cages. And when she saw Jorindel she was very angry, and screamed with rage; but she could not come within two yards of him; for the flower he held in his hand protected him. He looked around at the

The flower he held protected him

birds, but alas! there were many many nightingales, and how then should he find his Jorinda? While he was thinking what to do, he observed that the fairy had taken down one of the cages, and was making her escape through the door. He ran towards her, touched the cage with the flower, and his Jorinda stood before him. She threw her arms round his neck and looked as beautiful as ever, as beautiful as when they walked together in the wood.

Then he touched all the other birds with the flower, so that they again became young girls; and took his dear Jorinda home, where they lived happily together for many many years.

FREDERICK AND CATHERINE

THERE was once a man called Frederick: he had a wife whose name was Catherine, and they had not long been married. One day Frederick said, "Kate! I am going to work in the fields; when I come back I shall be hungry, so let me have something nice cooked, and a good draught of ale." "Very well," said she, "it shall all be ready." When dinner-time drew nigh, Catherine took a nice steak, which was all the meat she had, and put it on the fire to fry. The steak soon began to look brown, and to crackle in the pan; and Catherine stood by with a fork and turned it: then she said to herself, "The steak is almost ready, I may as well go to the cellar for the ale." So she left the pan on the fire, and took a large jug and went into the cellar and tapped the ale cask. The beer ran into the jug, and Catherine stood looking on. At last it popped into her head, "The dog is not shut up – he may be running away with the steak; that's well thought of." So up she ran from the cellar; and sure enough the rascally cur had got the steak in his mouth, and was making off with it.

Away ran Catherine, and away ran the dog across the field! But he ran faster than she, and stuck close to the steak. "It's all gone, and 'what can't be cursed must be endured,'" said Catherine. So she turned round; and as she had run a good way and was tired, she walked home leisurely to cool herself.

Now all this time the ale was running too, for Catherine had not turned the cock; and when the jug was full the liquor ran upon the floor till the cask was empty. When she got to the cellar stairs she saw what had happened. "My stars!" said she. "What shall I do to keep Frederick from seeing all this slopping about?" So she thought a while; and at last remembered that there was a sack of fine meal bought at the last fair, and that if she sprinkled this over the floor it would suck up the ale nicely. "What a lucky thing," said she, "that we kept that meal! We have now a good use for it." So away she went for it: but she managed to set it down just upon the great jug full of beer, and upset it; and thus all the ale that had been saved was set swimming on the floor also. "Ah! well," said she, "when one goes, another may as well follow." Then she strewed the meal all about the cellar, and was quite pleased with her cleverness, and said, "How very neat and clean it looks!"

At noon Frederick came home. "Now, wife," cried he, "what have you for dinner?" "O Frederick!" answered she. "I was cooking you a steak; but while I went down to draw the ale, the dog ran away with it; and while I ran after him, the ale all ran out; and when I went to dry up the ale with the sack of meal that we got at the fair, I upset the jug: but the cellar is now quite dry, and looks so clean!" "Kate, Kate," said he, "how could you do all this? Why did you leave the steak to fry, and the ale to run, and then spoil all the meal?" "Why, Frederick," said she, "I did not know I was doing wrong, you should have told me before."

The husband thought to himself, If my wife manages matters thus, I must look sharp myself. Now he had a good deal of gold in the house: so he said to Catherine, "What pretty yellow buttons these are! I shall put them into a box and bury them in the garden; but take care that you never go near or meddle with them." "No, Frederick," said she, "that I never will." As soon as he was gone, there came by some pedlars with earthenware plates and dishes, and they asked her whether she would buy. "Oh dear me, I should like to buy very much, but I have no money: if you had any use for yellow buttons, I might deal with you." "Yellow buttons!" said they. "Let us have a look at them." "Go into the garden and dig where I tell you, and you will find the yellow buttons: I dare not go myself." So the rogues went: and when they found what these yellow buttons were, they took them all away, and left her plenty of plates and dishes. Then she set them all about the house for a show: and when Frederick came back, he cried out, "Kate, what have you been doing?" "See," said she, "I have bought all these with your yellow buttons: but I did not touch them myself; the pedlars went themselves and dug them up." "Wife, wife," said Frederick, "what a pretty piece of work you have made! Those yellow buttons were all my money. How came you to do such a thing?" "Why," answered she, "I did not know there was any harm in it; you should have told me."

Catherine stood musing for a while, and at last said to her husband, "Hark ye, Frederick, we will soon get the gold back: let us run after the thieves." "Well, we will try," answered he; "but take some butter and cheese with you, that we may have something to eat by the way." "Very well," said she; and they set out: and as Frederick walked the fastest, he left his wife some way behind. "It does not matter," thought she. "When we turn back, I shall be so much nearer home than he."

Presently she came to the top of a hill, down the side of which there was a road so narrow that the cartwheels always chafed the trees on each side as they passed. "Ah, see now," said she, "how they have bruised and wounded those poor trees; they will never get well." So she took pity on them, and made use of the butter to grease them all, so that the wheels might not hurt them so much. While she was doing this kind office, one of her cheeses fell out of the basket, and rolled down the hill. Catherine looked, but could not see where it was gone; so she said, "Well, I suppose the other will go the same way and find you; he has younger legs than I have." Then she rolled the other cheese after it; and away it went, nobody knows where, down the hill. But she said she supposed they knew the road, and would follow her, and she could not stay there all day waiting for them.

At last she overtook Frederick, who desired her to give him something to eat. Then she gave him the dry bread. "Where are the butter and cheese?" said he. "Oh!" answered she. "I used the butter to grease those poor trees that the wheels chafed so: and one of the cheeses ran away, so I sent the other after it to find it, and I suppose they are both on the road together somewhere." "What a goose you are to do such silly things!" said the husband. "How can you say so?" said she. "I am sure you never told me not."

They ate the dry bread together; and Frederick said, "Kate, I hope you locked the door safe when you came away." "No," answered she, "you did not tell me." "Then go home, and do it now before we go any farther," said Frederick, "and bring with you something to eat."

Catherine did as he told her, and thought to herself by the way, "Frederick wants something to eat; but I don't think he is very fond of butter and cheese: I'll bring him a bag of fine nuts, and the vinegar, for I have often seen him take some."

When she reached home, she bolted the back door, but the front door she took off the hinges, and said, "Frederick told me to lock the door, but surely it can nowhere be so safe as if I take it with me." So she took her time by the way: and when she overtook her husband she cried out, "There, Frederick, there is the door itself, now you may watch it as carefully as you please." "Alas! alas!" said he. "What a clever wife I have! I sent you to make the house fast, and you take the door away, so that everybody may go in and out as they please: however, as you have brought the door, you shall carry it about with you for your pains." "Very well," answered she, "I'll carry the door; but I'll not carry the nuts and vinegar bottle also, that would be too much of a load; so, if you please, I'll fasten them to the door."

"I'll fasten them to the door," said Catherine

Frederick of course made no objection to that plan, and they set off into the wood to look for the thieves; but they could not find them: and when it grew dark, they climbed up into a tree to spend the night there. Scarcely were they up, than who should come by but the very rogues they were looking for. They were in truth great rascals, and belonged to that class of people who find things before they are lost. They were tired; so they sat down and made a fire under the very tree where Frederick and Catherine were. Frederick slipped

down on the other side, and picked up some stones.
Then he climbed up again, and tried to hit the
thieves on the head with them: but they only said,
"It must be near morning, for the wind shakes the
fir-apples down."

Catherine, who had the door on her shoulder,
began to be very tired; but she thought it was the
nuts upon it that were so heavy so she said softly,
"Frederick, I must let the nuts go." "No," answered
he, "not now, they will discover us." "I can't help
that, they must go." "Well then, make haste and
throw them down, if you will." Then away rattled
the nuts down among the boughs; and one of the
thieves cried, "Bless me, it is hailing."

A little while after, Catherine thought the door
was still very heavy: so she whispered to Frederick,
"I must throw the vinegar down." "Pray don't,"
answered he. "It will discover us." "I can't help
that," said she, "go it must." So she poured all the
vinegar down; and the thieves said, "What a heavy
dew there is!"

At last it popped into Catherine's head that it
was the door itself that was so heavy all the time:
so she whispered to Frederick, "I must throw the

door down soon." But he begged and prayed her not to do so, for he was sure it would betray them. "Here goes, however," said she: and down went the door with such a clatter upon the thieves, that they cried out "Murder!" and not knowing what was coming, ran away as fast as they could, and left all the gold. So when Frederick and Catherine came down, there they found all their money safe and sound.

THE THREE CHILDREN OF FORTUNE

ONCE upon a time a father sent for his three sons, and gave to the eldest a cock, to the second a scythe, and to the third a cat. "I am now old," said he, "my end is approaching, and I would fain provide for you before I die. Money I have none, and what I now give you seems of but little worth; yet it rests with yourselves alone to turn my gifts to good account. Only seek out a land where what you have is as yet unknown, and your fortune is made."

After the death of the father, the eldest set out with his cock: but wherever he went, in every town he saw from afar off a cock sitting upon the church steeple, and turning round with the wind. In the villages he always heard plenty of them crowing, and his bird was therefore nothing new; so there did not seem much chance of his making his fortune. At length it happened that he came to an island where the people who lived there had never heard of a cock, and knew not even how to reckon the time. They knew, indeed, if it were morning or evening; but at night, if they lay awake, they had no means of knowing how time went. "Behold," said he to them, "what a noble animal this is! How like a knight he is! He carries a bright red crest upon his head, and spurs upon his heels; he crows three times every night, at stated hours, and at the third time the sun is about to rise. But this is not all; sometimes he screams in broad daylight, and then you must take warning, for the weather is surely about to change."

This pleased the natives mightily; they kept awake one whole night, and heard, to their great joy, how gloriously the cock called the hour, at two, four, and six o'clock. Then they asked him whether the bird was to be sold, and how much he would sell it for. "About as much gold as an ass can carry," said he. "A very fair price for such an

animal," cried they with one voice; and agreed to
give him what he asked.

When he returned home with his wealth, his
brothers wondered greatly; and the second said, "I
will now set forth likewise, and see if I can turn my
scythe to as good an account." There did not seem,
however, much likelihood of this; for go where he
would, he was met by peasants who had as good a
scythe on their shoulders as he had. But at last, as
good luck would have it, he came to an island
where the people had never heard of a scythe: there,
as soon as the corn was ripe, they went into the
fields and pulled it up; but this was very hard work,
and a great deal of it was lost. The man then set to
work with his scythe; and mowed down their
whole crop so quickly, that the people stood staring
open-mouthed with wonder. They were willing to
give him what he asked for such a marvellous
thing: but he only took a horse laden with as much
gold as it could carry.

Now the third brother had a great longing to
go and see what he could make of his cat. So he set
out: and at first it happened to him as it had to the
others, so long as he kept upon the mainland, he

met with no success; there were plenty of cats everywhere, indeed too many, so that the young ones were for the most part, as soon as they came into the world, drowned in the water. At last he passed over to an island, where, as it chanced most luckily for him, nobody had ever seen a cat; and they were overrun with mice to such a degree, that the little wretches danced upon the tables and chairs, whether the master of the house were at home or not. The people complained loudly of this grievance; the king himself knew not how to rid himself of them in his palace; in every corner mice were squeaking, and they gnawed everything that their teeth could lay hold of. Here was a fine field for Puss – she soon began her chase, and had cleared two rooms in the twinkling of an eye; when the people besought their king to buy the wonderful animal, for the good of the public, at any price, the king willingly gave what was asked – a mule laden with gold and jewels; and thus the third brother returned home with a richer prize than either of the others.

Meantime the cat feasted away upon the mice in the royal palace, and devoured so many that they were no longer in any great numbers. At length, quite spent and tired with her work, she became extremely thirsty; so she stood still, drew up her head, and cried, "Miau, Miau!" The king gathered together all his subjects when they heard this strange cry, and many ran shrieking in a great fright out of the palace. But the king held a great council below as to what was best to be done; and it was at length fixed to send a herald to the cat, to warn her to leave the castle forthwith, or that force would be used to remove her. "For," said the councillors, "we would far more willingly put up with the mice (since we are used to that evil), than get rid of them at the risk of our lives." A page accordingly went, and asked the cat whether she were willing to quit the castle. But Puss, whose thirst became every moment more and more pressing, answered nothing but "Miau! Miau!" which the page interpreted to mean "No! No!" and therefore carried this answer to the king. "Well," said the councillors, "then we must try what force will do." So the guns were planted, and the palace was fired upon from all sides. When the fire reached the room where the cat was, she sprang out of the window and ran away; but the besiegers did not see her, and went on firing until the whole palace was burnt to the ground.

KING GRISLY-BEARD

A GREAT king had a daughter who was very beautiful, but so proud and haughty and conceited, that none of the princes who came to ask her in marriage was good enough for her, and she only made sport of them.

The time came when the king held a great feast, and invited all her suitors; and they sat in a row according to their rank, kings and princes and dukes and earls. Then the princess came in and passed by them all, but she had something spiteful to say to everyone. The first was too fat: "He's as round as a tub," said she. The next was too tall: "What a maypole!" said she. The next was too short: "What a dumpling!" said she. The fourth was too pale, and

she called him "Wallface". The fifth was too red, so
she called him "Cockscomb". The sixth was not
straight enough, so she said he was like a greenstick
that had been laid to dry over a baker's oven. And
thus she had some joke to crack upon everyone: but
she laughed more than all at a good king who was
there. "Look at him," said she. "His beard is like an
old mop, he shall be called Grisly-beard." So the
king got the nickname of Grisly-beard.

But the old king was very angry when he saw
how his daughter behaved, and how she ill-treated
all his guests; and he vowed that, willing or unwilling, she should marry the first beggar that came to
the door.

Two days after there came by a travelling
musician, who began to sing under the window,
and beg alms: and when the king heard him, he
said, "Let him come in." So they brought in a
dirty-looking fellow; and when he had sung before
the king and the princess, he begged a boon. Then
the king said, "You have sung so well, that I will
give you my daughter for your wife." The princess
begged and prayed; but the king said, "I have sworn
to give you to the first beggar, and I will keep my

word." So words and tears were of no avail; the parson was sent for, and she was married to the musician. When this was over, the king said, "Now get ready to go; you must not stay here; you must travel on with your husband."

Then the beggar departed, and took her with him; and they soon came to a great wood. "Pray," said she, "whose is this wood?" "It belongs to King Grisly-beard," answered he; "hadst thou taken him, all had been thine." "Ah! Unlucky wretch that I am!" sighed she. "Would that I had married King Grisly-beard!" Next they came to some fine meadows. "Whose are these beautiful green meadows?" said she. "They belong to King Grisly-beard; hadst thou taken him, they had all been thine." "Ah! Unlucky wretch that I am!" said she. "Would that I had married King Grisly-Beard!"

Then they came to a great city. "Whose is this noble city?" said she. "It belongs to King Grisly-beard; hadst thou taken him, it had all been thine." "Ah! Miserable wretch that I am!" sighed she. "Why did I not marry King Grisly-beard?" "That is no business of mine," said the musician. "Why should you wish for another husband? Am not I good enough for you?"

At last they came to a small cottage. "What a paltry place!" said she. "To whom does that little dirty hole belong?" The musician answered, "That is your and my house, where we are to live." "Where are your servants?" cried she. "What do we want with servants?" said he. "You must do for yourself whatever is to be done. Now make the fire, and put on water and cook my supper, for I am very tired." But the princess knew nothing of making fires and cooking, and the beggar was forced to help her. When they had eaten a very scanty meal they went to bed; but the musician called her up very early in the morning to clean the house. Thus they lived for two days: and when they had eaten up all there was in the cottage, the man said, "Wife, we can't go on thus, spending money and earning nothing. You must learn to weave baskets." Then he went out and cut willows and brought them home, and she began to weave: but it made her fingers very sore. "I see this work won't do," said he. "Try to spin; perhaps you will do that better." So she sat down and tried to spin; but the threads cut her tender fingers till the blood ran. "See now," said the musician, "you are good for nothing, you can do no work; what a bargain I have got! However, I'll try and set up a trade in pots and pans, and you shall stand in the market and sell them." "Alas!" sighed she. "When I stand in the market and any of my father's court pass by and see me there, how they will laugh at me!"

But the beggar did not care for that; and said she must work, if she did not wish to die of hunger. At first the trade went well; for many people, seeing such a beautiful woman, went to buy her wares, and paid their money without thinking of taking away the goods. They lived on this as long as it lasted, and then her husband bought a fresh lot of ware, and she sat herself down with it in a corner of the market; but a drunken soldier soon came by, and rode his horse against her stall and broke all her goods into a thousand pieces. Then she began to weep, and knew not what to do. "Ah! what will become of me!" said she. "What will my husband say?" So she ran home and told him all. "Who would have thought you would have been so silly," said he, "as to put an earthenware stall in the corner of the market, where everybody passes? But let us have no more crying; I see you are not fit for this sort of work: so I have been to the king's palace, and asked if they did not want a kitchen-maid, and they have promised to take you, and there you will have plenty to eat."

Thus the princess became a kitchen-maid, and helped the cook to do all the dirtiest work; she was allowed to carry home some of the meat that was left, and on this she and her husband lived.

She had not been there long, before she heard that the king's eldest son was passing by, going to be married; and she went to one of the windows and looked out. Everything was ready, and all the pomp and splendour of the court was there. Then she thought with an aching heart on her own sad fate, and bitterly grieved for the pride and folly which had brought her so low. And the servants gave her some of the rich meats, which she put into her basket to take home.

All on a sudden, as she was going out, in came the king's son in golden clothes: and when he saw a beautiful woman at the door, he took her by the hand, and said she should be his partner in the dance: but she trembled for fear, for she saw that it was King Grisly-beard, who was making sport of her. However, he kept fast hold and led her in; and the cover of the basket came off, so that the meats in it fell all about. Then everybody laughed and jeered at her; and she was so abashed that she wished herself a thousand feet deep in the earth. She sprang to the door to run away; but on the steps King Grisly-beard overtook and brought her back, and said, "Fear me not! I am the musician who has lived with you in the hut: I brought you there because I loved you. I am also the soldier who overset your stall. I have done all this only to cure you of pride, and to punish you for the ill-treatment you bestowed on me. Now all is over; you have learnt wisdom, your faults are gone, and it is time to celebrate our marriage feast!"

Then the chamberlains came and brought her the most beautiful robes: and her father and his whole court were there already, and congratulated her on her marriage. Joy was in every face. The feast was grand, and all were merry; and I wish you and I had been of the party.

SNOW-DROP

IT was in the middle of winter, when the broad flakes of snow were falling around, that a certain queen sat working at a window, the frame of which was made of fine black ebony; and as she was looking out upon the snow, she pricked her finger, and three drops of blood fell upon it. Then she gazed thoughtfully upon the red drops which sprinkled the white snow, and said, "Would that my little daughter may be as white as that snow, as red as the blood, and as black as the ebony window frame!" And so the little girl grew up: her skin was as white as snow, her cheeks as rosy as the blood, and her hair as black as ebony; and she was called Snow-drop.

But this queen died; and the king soon married another wife, who was very beautiful, but so proud that she could not bear to think that anyone could surpass her. She had a magical looking glass, to which she used to go and gaze upon herself in it, and say,

> "Tell me, glass, tell me true!
> Of all the ladies in the land,
> Who is the fairest? Tell me who?"

And the glass answered,

> "Thou, queen, art fairest in the land."

But Snow-drop grew more and more beautiful; and when she was seven years old, she was as bright as the day, and fairer than the queen herself. Then the glass one day answered the queen, when she went to consult it as usual,

> "Thou, queen, may'st fair and beauteous be,
> But Snow-drop is lovelier far than thee!"

When she heard this, she turned pale with rage and envy; and called to one of her servants and said, "Take Snow-drop away into the wide wood, that I may never see her more." Then the servant led her away; but his heart melted when she begged him to spare her life, and he said, "I will not hurt thee, thou pretty child." So he left her by herself; and though he thought it most likely that the wild beasts would tear her in pieces, he felt as if a great weight were taken off his heart when he had made up his mind not to kill her, but leave her to her fate.

Then poor Snow-drop wandered along through the wood in great fear; and the wild beasts roared about her, but none did her any harm. In the evening she came to a little cottage, and went in there to rest herself, for her little feet would carry her no farther. Everything was spruce and neat in the cottage: on the table was spread a white cloth, and there were seven little plates with seven little loaves, and seven little glasses with wine in them; and knives and forks laid in order; and by the wall stood seven little beds. Then, as she was very hungry, she picked up a little piece off each loaf, and drank a very little wine out of each glass; and after that she thought she would lie down and rest. So she tried all the little beds; and one was too long, and another was too short, till at last the seventh suited her; and there she laid herself down, and went to sleep.

Presently in came the masters of the cottage, who were seven little dwarfs that lived among the mountains, and dug and searched for gold. They lighted up their seven lamps, and saw directly that all was not right. The first said, "Who has been sitting on my stool?" The second, "Who has been eating off my plate?" The third, "Who has been picking my bread?" The fourth, "Who has been meddling with my spoon?" The fifth, "Who has been handling my fork?" The sixth, "Who has been cutting with my knife?" The seventh, "Who has been drinking my wine?" Then the first looked round and said, "Who has been lying on my bed?" And the rest came running to him, and everyone cried out that somebody had been upon his bed. But the seventh saw Snow-drop, and called all his brethren to come and see her; and they cried out with wonder and astonishment, and brought their lamps to look at her, and said, "Good heavens! What a lovely child she is!" And they were delighted to see her, and took care not to wake her; and the seventh dwarf slept an hour

Snow-drop fell down senseless (Snow-drop)

with each of the other dwarfs in turn, till the night
was gone.

In the morning, Snow-drop told them all her
story; and they pitied her, and said if she would
keep all things in order, and cook and wash, and
knit and spin for them, she might stay where she
was, and they would take good care of her. Then
they went out all day long to their work, seeking
for gold and silver in the mountains; and Snow-
drop remained at home: and they warned her, and
said, "The queen will soon find out where you are,
so take care and let no one in."

But the queen, now that she thought Snow-
drop was dead, believed that she was certainly the
handsomest lady in the land; and she went to her
glass and said,

> "Tell me, glass, tell me true!
>   Of all the ladies in the land,
> Who is fairest? Tell me who?"

And the glass answered,

> "Thou, queen, art the fairest in all this land;
> But over the hills, in the greenwood shade,

Where the seven dwarfs their dwelling have made,
There Snow-drop is hiding her head, and she
Is lovelier far, O queen! than thee."

Then the queen was very much alarmed; for
she knew that the glass always spoke the truth, and
was sure that the servant had betrayed her. And she
could not bear to think that anyone lived who was
more beautiful than she was; so she disguised
herself as an old pedlar, and went her way over the
hills to the place where the dwarfs dwelt. Then she
knocked at the door, and cried "Fine wares to sell!"
Snow-drop looked out at the window, and said,
"Good-day, good woman; what have you to sell?"
"Good wares, fine wares," said she; "laces and
bobbins of all colours." "I will let the old lady in;
she seems to be a very good sort of body," thought
Snow-drop; so she ran down, and unbolted the
door. "Bless me!" said the old woman. "How badly
your stays are laced! Let me lace them up with one
of my nice new laces." Snow-drop did not dream
of any mischief; so she stood up before the old
woman; but she set to work so nimbly, and pulled
the lace so tight, that Snow-drop lost her breath,

and fell down as if she were dead. "There's an end of all thy beauty," said the spiteful queen, and went away home.

In the evening the seven dwarfs returned; and I need not say how grieved they were to see their faithful Snow-drop stretched upon the ground motionless, as if she were quite dead. However, they lifted her up, and when they found what was the matter, they cut the lace; and in a little time she began to breathe, and soon came to life again. Then they said, "The old woman was the queen herself; take care another time, and let no one in when we are away."

When the queen got home, she went straight to her glass, and spoke to it as usual; but to her great surprise it still said,

"Thou, queen, art the fairest in all this land;
But over the hills, in the greenwood shade,
Where the seven dwarfs their dwelling have made,
There Snow-drop is hiding her head, and she
Is lovelier far, O queen! than thee."

Then the blood ran cold in her heart with spite and malice to see that Snow-drop still lived; and she dressed herself up again in a disguise, but very different from the one she wore before, and took with her a poisoned comb. When she reached the dwarfs' cottage, she knocked at the door, and cried "Fine wares to sell!" But Snow-drop said, "I dare not let anyone in." Then the queen said, "Only look at my beautiful combs;" and gave her the poisoned one. And it looked so pretty that she took it up and put it into her hair to try it; but the moment it touched her head the poison was so powerful that she fell down senseless. "There you may lie," said the queen, and went her way. But by good luck the dwarfs returned very early that evening; and when they saw Snow-drop lying on the ground, they thought what had happened, and soon found the poisoned comb. And when they took it away, she recovered, and told them all that had passed; and they warned her once more not to open the door to anyone.

Meantime the queen went home to her glass, and trembled with rage when she received exactly the same answer as before; and she said, "Snow-drop shall die, if it costs me my life." So she went secretly into a chamber, and prepared a poisoned apple: the outside looked very rosy and tempting, but whoever tasted it was sure to die. Then she dressed herself up as a peasant's wife, and travelled over the hills to the dwarfs' cottage, and knocked at the door; but Snow-drop put her head out of the window and said, "I dare not let anyone in, for the dwarfs have told me not." "Do as you please," said the old woman, "but at any rate take this pretty apple; I will make you a present of it." "No," said Snow-drop, "I dare not take it." "You silly girl!" answered the other. "What are you afraid of? Do you think it is poisoned? Come! Do you eat one part, and I will eat the other." Now the apple was so prepared that one side was good, though the other side was poisoned. Then Snow-drop was very much tempted to taste, for the apple looked exceedingly nice; and when she saw the old woman eat, she could refrain no longer. But she had scarcely put the piece into her mouth, when she fell down dead upon the ground. "This time nothing will save thee," said the queen; and she went home to her glass, and at last it said,

"Thou, queen, art the fairest of all the fair."

And then her envious heart was glad, and as happy as such a heart could be.

When evening came, and the dwarfs returned home, they found Snow-drop lying on the ground: no breath passed her lips, and they were afraid that she was quite dead. They lifted her up, and combed her hair, and washed her face with wine and water; but all was in vain, for the little girl seemed quite dead. So they laid her down upon a bier, and then they proposed to bury her: but her cheeks were still rosy, and her face looked just as it did while she was alive; so they said, "We will never bury her in the cold ground." And they made a coffin of glass, so that they might still look at her, and wrote her name upon it, in golden letters, and that she was a king's daughter. And the coffin was placed upon the hill, and one of the dwarfs always sat by it and watched. And the birds of the air came too, and bemoaned Snow-drop: first of all came an owl, and then a raven, but at last came a dove.

And thus Snow-drop lay for a long long time,

and still only looked as though she were asleep; for she was even now as white as snow, and as red as blood, and as black as ebony. At last a prince came and called at the dwarfs' house; and he saw Snow-drop, and read what was written in golden letters. Then he offered the dwarfs money, and earnestly prayed them to let him take her away; but they said, "We will not part with her for all the gold in the world." At last however they had pity on him, and gave him the coffin: but the moment he lifted it up to carry it home with him, the piece of apple fell from between her lips, and Snow-drop awoke, and said, "Where am I?" And the prince answered, "Thou art safe with me." Then he told her all that had happened, and said, "I love you better than all the world: come with me to my father's palace, and you shall be my wife." And Snow-drop consented, and went home with the prince; and everything was prepared with great pomp and splendour for their wedding.

To the feast was invited, among the rest, Snow-drop's old enemy the queen; and as she was dressing herself in fine rich clothes, she looked in the glass, and said,

"Tell me, glass, tell me true!
Of all the ladies in the land,
Who is fairest? Tell me who?"

And the glass answered,

"Thou, lady, art loveliest *here*, I ween;
But lovelier far is the new-made queen."

When she heard this, she burned with rage; but her envy and curiosity were so great, that she could not help setting out to see the bride. And when she arrived, and saw that it was no other than Snow-drop, who, as she thought, had been dead a long while, she choked with passion, and fell ill and died; but Snow-drop and the prince lived and reigned happily over that land many many years.

THE ELVES AND THE SHOEMAKER

THERE was once a shoemaker who worked very
hard and was very honest; but still he could not
earn enough to live upon, and at last all he had in
the world was gone, except just leather enough to
make one pair of shoes. Then he cut them all ready
to make up the next day, meaning to get up early
in the morning to work. His conscience was clear
and his heart light amidst all his troubles; so he
went peaceably to bed, left all his cares to heaven,
and fell asleep. In the morning, after he had said his
prayers, he set himself down to his work, when, to
his great wonder, there stood the shoes, all ready
made, upon the table. The good man knew not
what to say or think of this strange event. He

looked at the workmanship; there was not one false stitch in the whole job; and all was so neat and true, that it was a complete masterpiece.

That same day a customer came in, and the shoes pleased him so well that he willingly paid a price higher than usual for them; and the poor shoemaker bought with the money leather enough to make two pairs more. In the evening he cut out the work, and went to bed early that he might get up and begin betimes next day: but he was saved all the trouble, for when he got up in the morning the work was finished ready to his hand. Presently in came buyers, who paid him handsomely for his goods, so that he bought leather enough for four pairs more. He cut out the work again over night, and found it finished in the morning as before; and so it went on for some time: what was got ready in the evening was always done by daybreak, and the good man soon became thriving and prosperous again.

One evening about Christmas time, as he and his wife were sitting over the fire chatting together, he said to her, "I should like to sit up and watch tonight, that we may see who it is that comes and does my work for me." The wife liked the thought; so they left a light burning, and hid themselves in the corner of the room behind a curtain that was hung up there, and watched what should happen.

As soon as it was midnight, there came two little naked dwarfs; and they sat themselves upon the shoemaker's bench, took up all the work that was cut out, and began to ply with their little fingers, stitching and rapping and tapping away at such a rate, that the shoemaker was all amazement, and could not take his eyes off for a moment. And on they went till the job was quite finished, and the shoes stood ready for use upon the table. This was long before daybreak; and then they bustled away as quick as lightning.

The next day the wife said to the shoemaker, "These little wights have made us rich, and we ought to be thankful to them, and do them a good office in return. I am quite vexed to see them run about as they do; they have nothing upon their backs to keep off the cold. I'll tell you what, I will make each of them a shirt, and a coat and waistcoat, and a pair of pantaloons into the bargain; do you make each of them a little pair of shoes."

They danced and capered and sprang about

The thought pleased the good shoemaker very much; and one evening, when all the things were ready, they laid them on the table instead of the work that they used to cut out, and then went and hid themselves to watch what the little elves would do. About midnight they came in, and were going to sit down to their work as usual; but when they saw the clothes lying for them, they laughed and were greatly delighted. Then they dressed themselves in the twinkling of an eye, and danced and capered and sprang about as merry as could be, till at last they danced out at the door over the green; and the shoemaker saw them no more: but everything went well with him from that time forward, as long as he lived.

THE LADY AND THE LION

A MERCHANT, who had three daughters, was once setting out upon a journey; but before he went he asked each daughter what gift he should bring back for her. The eldest wished for pearls; the second for jewels; but the third said, "Dear father, bring me a rose." Now it was no easy task to find a rose, for it was the middle of winter; yet, as she was the fairest daughter, and was very fond of flowers, her father said he would try what he could do. So he kissed all three, and bid them goodbye. And when the time came for his return, he had bought pearls and jewels for the two eldest, but he had sought everywhere in vain for the rose; and when he went into any garden and inquired for such a thing, the people laughed at him, and asked him whether he thought roses grew in snow. This grieved him very much, for his third daughter was his dearest child. But as he was journeying home, thinking what he should bring her, he came to a fine castle; and around the castle was a garden, in half of which it appeared to be summertime, and in the other half winter. On one side the finest flowers were in full bloom, and on the other everything looked desolate and buried in snow. "A lucky hit!" said he as he called to his servant, and told him to go to a beautiful bed of roses that was there, and bring him away one of the flowers. This done, they were riding away well pleased, when a fierce lion sprang up, and roared out, "Whoever dares to steal my roses shall be eaten up alive." Then the man said, "I knew not that the garden belonged to you; can nothing save my life?" "No!" said the lion. "Nothing, unless you promise to give me whatever meets you first on your return home; if you agree to this, I will give you your life, and the rose too for your daughter." But the man was unwilling to do so, and said, "It may be my youngest daughter, who loves me most, and always runs to meet me when I go home." Then the servant was greatly frightened, and said, "It may perhaps be only a cat or a dog." And at last the man yielded with a heavy heart, and took the rose; and promised the lion whatever should meet him first on his return.

And as he came near home, it was his youngest and dearest daughter that met him; she came running and kissed him, and welcomed him home; and when she saw that he had brought her the rose, she rejoiced still more. But her father began to be very melancholy, and to weep, saying, "Alas, my dearest child! I have bought this flower dear, for I have promised to give you to a wild lion, and when he has you, he will tear you in pieces, and eat you." And he told her all that had happened; and said she should not go, let what would happen.

But she comforted him, and said, "Dear father, what you have promised must be fulfilled; I will go to the lion, and soothe him, that he may let me return again safe home."

The next morning she asked the way she was to go, and took leave of her father, and went forth with a bold heart into the wood. But the lion was an enchanted prince: by day he and all his court

The lady calls upon the winds
(The Lady and the Lion)

were lions, but in the evening they took their proper forms again. And when the lady came to the castle, he welcomed her so courteously that she consented to marry him. The wedding feast was held, and they lived happily together a long time. The prince was only to be seen as soon as evening came, and then he held his court; but every morning he left his bride, and went away by himself, she knew not whither, till night came again.

After some time he said to her, "Tomorrow there will be a great feast in your father's house, for your eldest sister is to be married; and, if you wish to go to visit her, my lions shall lead you thither." Then she rejoiced much at the thought of seeing her father once more, and set out with the lions; and everyone was overjoyed to see her, for they had thought her dead long since. But she told them how happy she was; and stayed till the feast was over, and then went back to the wood.

Her second sister was soon after married; and when she was invited to the wedding, she said to the prince, "I will not go alone this time; you must go with me." But he would not, and said that would be a very hazardous thing, for if the least ray

of the torchlight should fall upon him, his enchantment would become still worse, for he should be
changed into a dove, and be obliged to wander
about the world for seven long years. However,
she gave him no rest, and said she would take care
no light should fall upon him. So at last they set
out together, and took with them their little child
too; and she chose a large hall with thick walls for
him to sit in while the wedding torches were
lighted; but unluckily no one observed that there
was a crack in the door. Then the wedding was
held with great pomp; but as the train came from
the church, and passed with the torches before the
hall, a very small ray of light fell upon the prince.
In a moment he disappeared; and when his wife
came in, and sought him, she found only a white
dove. Then he said to her, "Seven years must I fly
up and down over the face of the earth; but every
now and then I will let fall a white feather, that
shall show you the way I am going; follow it, and
at last you may overtake and set me free."

This said, he flew out at the door, and she
followed; and every now and then a white feather
fell, and showed her the way she was to journey.

Thus she went roving on through the wide world, and looked neither to the right hand nor to the left, nor took any rest for seven years. Then she began to rejoice, and thought to herself that the time was fast coming when all her troubles should cease; yet repose was still far off: for one day as she was travelling on, she missed the white feather, and when she lifted up her eyes she could nowhere see the dove. "Now," thought she to herself, "no human aid can be of use to me;" so she went to the sun, and said, "Thou shinest everywhere, on the mountain's top, and the valley's depth; hast thou anywhere seen a white dove?" "No," said the sun, "I have not seen it; but I will give thee a casket – open it when thy hour of need comes." So she thanked the sun, and went on her way till eventide; and when the moon arose, she cried unto it, and said, "Thou shinest through all the night, over field and grove: hast thou nowhere seen a white dove?" "No," said the moon, "I cannot help thee; but I will give thee an egg – break it when need comes." Then she thanked the moon, and went on till the night wind blew; and she raised up her voice to it, and said, "Thou blowest through every tree and

under every leaf: has thou not seen the white dove?"
"No," said the night wind; "but I will ask three
other winds; perhaps they have seen it." Then the
east wind and the west wind came, and said they
too had not seen it; but the south wind said, "I have
seen the white dove; he has fled to the Red Sea, and
is changed once more into a lion, for the seven
years are passed away; and there he is fighting with
a dragon, and the dragon is an enchanted princess,
who seeks to separate him from you." Then the
night wind said, "I will give thee counsel. Go to
the Red Sea; on the right shore stand many reeds;
number them, and when thou comest to the eleventh, break it off and smite the dragon with it; so
the lion will have the victory, and both of them
will appear to you in their human forms. Then
instantly set out with thy beloved prince, and
journey home over sea and land."

So our poor wanderer went forth, and found
all as the night wind had said; and she plucked the
eleventh rod, and smote the dragon, and immediately the lion became a prince and the dragon a
princess again. But she forgot the counsel which
the night wind had given; and the false princess

watched her opportunity, and took the prince by the arm, and carried him away.

Thus the unfortunate traveller was again forsaken and forlorn; but she took courage and said, "As far as the wind blows, and so long as the cock crows, I will journey on till I find him once again." She went on for a long way, till at length she came to the castle whither the princess had carried the prince; and there was a feast prepared, and she heard that the wedding was about to be held. "Heaven aid me now!" said she; and she took the casket that the sun had given her, and found that within it lay a dress as dazzling as the sun itself. So she put it on, and went into the palace; and all the people gazed upon her; and the dress pleased the bride so much that she asked whether it was to be sold. "Not for gold and silver," answered the maiden; "but for flesh and blood." The princess asked what she meant; and she said, "Let me speak with the bridegroom this night in his chamber, and I will give thee the dress." At last, the princess agreed; but she told her chamberlain to give the prince a sleeping draught, that he might not hear or see her. When evening came, and the prince had fallen asleep, she was led into his chamber, and she sat herself down at his feet and said, "I have followed thee seven years; I have been to the sun, the moon, and the night wind, to seek thee; and at last I have helped thee to overcome the dragon. Wilt thou then forget me quite?" But the prince slept so soundly that her voice only passed over him, and seemed like the murmuring of the wind among the fir trees.

Then she was led away, and forced to give up the golden dress; and when she saw that there was no help for her, she went out into the meadow and sat herself down and wept. But as she sat she bethought herself of the egg that the moon had given her; and when she broke it, there ran out a hen and twelve chickens of pure gold, that played about, and then nestled under the old one's wings, so as to form the most beautiful sight in the world. And she rose up, and drove them before her till the bride saw them from her window, and was so pleased that she came forth, and asked her if she would sell the brood. "Not for gold or silver; but for flesh and blood: let me again this evening speak with the bridegroom in his chamber."

Then the princess thought to betray her as

before, and agreed to what she asked; but when the prince went to his chamber, he asked the chamberlain why the wind had murmured so in the night. And the chamberlain told him all; how he had given him a sleeping draught, and a poor maiden had come and spoken to him in his chamber, and was to come again that night. Then the prince took care to throw away the sleeping draught; and when she came and began again to tell him what woes had befallen her, and how faithful and true to him she had been, he knew his beloved wife's voice, and sprang up, and said, "You have awakened me as from a dream; for the strange princess had thrown a spell around me, so that I had altogether forgotten you: but heaven hath sent you to me in a lucky hour."

And they stole away out of the palace by night secretly (for they feared the princess), and journeyed home; and there they found their child, now grown comely and fair, and lived happily together to the end of their days.

THE KING OF THE
GOLDEN MOUNTAIN

A CERTAIN merchant had two children, a son and daughter, both very young, and scarcely able to run alone. He had two richly laden ships then making a voyage upon the seas, in which he had embarked all his property, in the hope of making great gains, when the news came that they were lost. Thus from being a rich man he became very poor, so that nothing was left him but one small plot of land; and, to relieve his mind a little of his trouble, he often went out to walk there.

One day, as he was roving along, a little rough-looking dwarf stood before him, and asked him why he was so sorrowful, and what it was that he took so deeply to heart. But the merchant replied,

"If you could do me any good, I would tell you."
"Who knows but I may?" said the little man. "Tell
me what is the matter, and perhaps I can be of
some service." Then the merchant told him how all
his wealth was gone to the bottom of the sea, and
how he had nothing left except that little plot of
land. "Oh! Trouble not yourself about that," said
the dwarf; "only promise to bring me here, twelve
years hence, whatever meets you first on your
return home, and I will give you as much gold as
you please." The merchant thought this was no
great request; that it would most likely be his dog,
or something of that sort, but forgot his little child:
so he agreed to the bargain, and signed and sealed
the engagement to do what was required.

But as he drew near home, his little boy was so
pleased to see him, that he crept behind him and
laid fast hold of his legs. Then the father started
with fear, and saw what it was that he had bound
himself to do; but as no gold was come, he consoled
himself by thinking that it was only a joke that the
dwarf was playing him.

About a month afterwards he went upstairs
into an old lumber room to look for some old iron,

that he might sell it and raise a little money; and there he saw a large pile of gold lying on the floor. At the sight of this he was greatly delighted, went into trade again, and became a greater merchant than before.

Meantime his son grew up, and as the end of the twelve years drew near, the merchant became very anxious and thoughtful, so that care and sorrow were written upon his face. The son one day asked what was the matter: but his father refused to tell for some time; at last however he said that he had, without knowing it, sold him to a little ugly-looking dwarf for a great quantity of gold; and that the twelve years were coming round when he must perform his agreement. Then the son said, "Father, give yourself very little trouble about that; depend upon it I shall be too much for the little man."

When the time came, they went out together to the appointed place; and the son drew a circle on the ground, and set himself and his father in the middle. The little dwarf soon came, and said to the merchant, "Have you brought me what you promised?" The old man was silent, but his son answered,

"What do you want here?" The dwarf said, "I come to talk with your father, not with you." "You have deceived and betrayed my father," said the son. "Give him up his bond." "No," replied the other, "I will not yield up my rights." Upon this a long dispute arose; and at last it was agreed that the son should be put into an open boat, that lay on the side of a piece of water hard by, and that the father should push him off with his own hand; so that he should be turned adrift. Then he took leave of his father, and set himself in the boat; and as it was pushed off it heaved, and fell on one side into the water: so the merchant thought that his son was lost, and went home very sorrowful.

But the boat went safely on, and did not sink; and the young man sat securely within, till at length it ran ashore upon an unknown land. As he jumped upon the shore, he saw before him a beautiful castle, but empty and desolate within, for it was enchanted. At last, however, he found a white snake in one of the chambers.

Now the white snake was an enchanted princess; and she rejoiced greatly to see him, and said, "Art thou at last come to be my deliverer? Twelve long years have I waited for thee, for thou alone canst save me. This night twelve men will come; their faces will be black, and they will be hung round with chains. They will ask what thou dost here; but be silent, give no answer, and let them do what they will – beat and torment thee. Suffer all, only speak not a word, and at twelve o'clock they must depart. The second night twelve others will come; and the third night twenty-four, who will even cut off thy head; but at the twelfth hour of that night their power is gone, and I shall be free, and will come and bring thee the water of life and health." And all came to pass as she had said; the merchant's son spoke not a word, and the third night the princess appeared, and fell on his neck and kissed him; joy and gladness burst forth throughout the castle; the wedding was celebrated, and he was king of the Golden Mountain.

They lived together very happily, and the queen had a son. Eight years had passed over their heads when the king thought of his father: and his heart was moved, and he longed to see him once again. But the queen opposed his going, and said, "I know well that misfortunes will come." However, he gave her no rest till she consented. At his departure, she presented him with a wishing ring, and said, "Take this ring, and put it on your finger; whatever you wish it will bring you: only promise that you will not make use of it to bring me hence to your father's." Then he promised what she asked, and put the ring on his finger, and wished himself near the town where his father lived. He found himself at the gates in a moment; but the guards would not let him enter, because he was so strangely clad. So he went up to a neighbouring mountain where a shepherd dwelt, and borrowed his old smock, and thus passed unobserved into the town. When he came to his father's house, he said he was his son; but the merchant would not believe him, and said he had had but one son, who he knew was long since dead; and as he was only dressed like a poor shepherd, he would not even offer him anything to eat. The king however persisted that he was his son, and said, "Is there no mark by which you would know if I am really your son?" "Yes," observed his mother, "our son has a mark like a raspberry under the right arm." Then he showed them the mark, and they were satisfied

that what he had said was true. He next told them
how he was king of the Golden Mountain, and was
married to a princess, and had a son seven years
old. But the merchant said, "That can never be
true; he must be a fine king truly who travels about
in a shepherd's smock." At this the son was very
angry; and, forgetting his promise, turned his ring,
and wished for his queen and son. In an instant they
stood before him; but the queen wept, and said
he had broken his word, and misfortune would
follow. He did all he could to soothe her, and she
at last appeared to be appeased; but she was not so
in reality, and only meditated how she should take
her revenge.

One day he took her to walk with him out of
the town, and showed her the spot where the boat
was turned adrift upon the wide waters. Then he
sat himself down, and said, "I am very much tired;
sit by me, I will rest my head in your lap, and sleep
a while." As soon as he had fallen asleep, however,
she drew the ring from his finger, and crept softly
away, and wished herself and her son at home in
their kingdom. And when the king awoke, he
found himself alone, and saw that the ring was

gone from his finger. "I can never return to my
father's house," said he; "they would say I am a
sorcerer; I will journey forth into the world till I
come again to my kingdom."

So saying, he set out and travelled till he came
to a mountain, where three giants were sharing
their inheritance; and as they saw him pass, they
cried out and said, "Little men have sharp wits; he
shall divide the inheritance between us." Now it
consisted of a sword that cut off an enemy's head
whenever the wearer gave the words "Heads off!";
a cloak that made the owner invisible, or gave him
any form he pleased; and a pair of boots that
transported the person who put them on wherever
he wished. The king said they must first let him try
these wonderful things, that he might know how
to set a value upon them. Then they gave him the
cloak, and he wished himself a fly, and in a moment
he was a fly. "The cloak is very well," said he.
"Now give me the sword." "No," said they, "not
unless you promise not to say 'Heads off!' for if
you do, we are all dead men." So they gave it him
on condition that he tried its virtue only on a tree.
He next asked for the boots also; and the moment

he had all three in his possession he wished himself at the Golden Mountain; and there he was in an instant. So the giants were left behind with no inheritance to divide or quarrel about.

As he came near to the castle he heard the sound of merry music; and the people around told him that his queen was about to celebrate her marriage with another prince. Then he threw his cloak around him, and passed through the castle, and placed himself by the side of his queen, where no one saw him. But when anything to eat was put upon her plate, he took it away and ate it himself; and when a glass of wine was handed to her, he took and drank it: and thus, though they kept on serving her with meat and drink, her plate continued always empty.

Upon this, fear and remorse came over her, and she went into her chamber and wept; and he followed her there. "Alas!" said she to herself. "Did not my deliverer come? why then doth enchantment still surround me?"

"Thou traitress!" said he. "Thy deliverer indeed came, and now is near thee: has he deserved this of thee?" And he went out and dismissed the company, and said the wedding was at an end, for that he was returned to his kingdom: but the princes and nobles and councillors mocked at him. However, he would enter into no parley with them, but only demanded whether they would depart in peace, or not. Then they turned and tried to seize him; but he drew his sword, and, with a word, the traitors' heads fell before him; and he was once more king of the Golden Mountain.

THE GOLDEN GOOSE

THERE was a man who had three sons. The youngest was called Dummling, and was on all occasions despised and ill-treated by the whole family. It happened that the eldest took it into his head one day to go into the wood to cut fuel; and his mother gave him a delicious pasty and a bottle of wine to take with him, that he might refresh himself at his work. As he went into the wood, a little old man bid him good day, and said, "Give me a little piece of meat from your plate, and a little wine out of your bottle; I am very hungry and thirsty." But this clever young man said, "Give you my meat and wine! No, I thank you; I should not have enough left for myself:" and away he went. He soon began to cut down a tree; but he had not worked long before he missed his stroke, and cut himself, and was obliged to go home to have the wound dressed. Now it was the little old man that caused him this mischief.

Next went the second son to work; and his mother gave him too a pasty and a bottle of wine. And the same little old man met him also, and asked him for something to eat and drink. But he too thought himself vastly clever, and said, "Whatever you get, I shall lose; so go your way!" The little man took care that he should have his reward; and the second stroke that he aimed against a tree, hit him on the leg; so that he too was forced to go home.

Then Dummling said, "Father, I should like to go and cut wood too." But his father answered, "Your brothers have both lamed themselves; you had better stay at home, for you know nothing of the business." But Dummling was very pressing; and at last his father said, "Go your way; you will be wiser when you have suffered for your folly." And his mother gave him only some dry bread, and a bottle of sour beer; but when he went into the wood, he met the little old man, who said, "Give me some meat and drink, for I am very hungry and thirsty." Dummling said, "I have only dry bread and sour beer; if that will suit you, we will sit down and eat it together." So they sat down; and when the lad pulled out his bread, behold it was turned into a capital pasty, and his sour beer became delightful wine. They ate and drank heartily; and when they had done, the little man said, "As you have a kind heart, and have been willing to share everything with me, I will send a blessing upon you. There stands an old tree; cut it down, and you will find something at the root." Then he took his leave, and went his way.

Dummling set to work, and cut down the tree; and when it fell, he found in a hollow under the roots a goose with feathers of pure gold. He took it up, and went on to an inn, where he proposed to sleep for the night. The landlord had three daughters; and when they saw the goose, they were very curious to examine what this wonderful bird could be, and wished very much to pluck one of the feathers out of its tail. At last the eldest said, "I must and will have a feather." So she waited till his back was turned, and then seized the goose by the wing; but to her great surprise there she stuck, for neither hand nor finger could she get away again. Presently in came the second sister, and thought to have a feather too; but the moment she touched her sister, there she too hung fast. At last came the third, and wanted a feather; but the other two cried out, "Keep away! For heaven's sake, keep away!" However, she did not understand what they meant. "If they are there," thought she, "I may well be there too." So she went up to them; but the moment she touched her sisters she stuck fast, and hung to the goose as they did. And so they kept company with the goose all night.

The next morning Dummling carried off the goose under his arm; and took no notice of the three girls, but went out with them sticking fast behind; and wherever he travelled, they too were obliged to follow, whether they would or no, as fast as their legs could carry them.

In the middle of a field the parson met them; and when he saw the train, he said, "Are you not ashamed of yourselves, you bold girls, to run after the young man in that way over the fields? Is that proper behaviour?" Then he took the youngest by the hand to lead her away; but the moment he touched her he too hung fast, and followed in the train. Presently up came the clerk; and when he saw his master the parson running after the three girls, he wondered greatly, and said, "Hollo, hollo, your reverence! Whither so fast? There is a christening today." Then he ran up, and took him by the gown, and in a moment he was fast too. As the five were thus trudging along, one behind another, they met two labourers with their mattocks coming from work; and the parson cried out to them to set him free. But scarcely had they touched him, when they too fell into the ranks, and so made seven, all running after Dummling and his goose.

At last they arrived at a city, where reigned a king who had an only daughter. The princess was of so thoughtful and serious a turn of mind that no one could make her laugh; and the king had proclaimed to all the world, that whoever could make her laugh should have her for his wife. When the young man heard this, he went to her with his goose and all its train; and as soon as she saw the seven all hanging together, and running about, treading on each other's heels, she could not help bursting into a long and loud laugh. Then Dummling claimed her for his wife; the wedding was celebrated, and he was heir to the kingdom, and lived long and happily with his wife.

MRS FOX

THERE was once a sly old fox with nine tails, who was very curious to know whether his wife was true to him: so he stretched himself out under a bench, and pretended to be as dead as a mouse.

Then Mrs Fox went up into her own room and locked the door: but her maid, the cat, sat at the kitchen fire cooking; and soon after it became known that the old fox was dead, someone knocked at the door, saying,

> "Miss Pussy! Miss Pussy! How fare you today?
> Are you sleeping or watching the time away?"

Then the cat went and opened the door, and there stood a young fox; so she said to him,

"No, no, Master Fox, I don't sleep in the day,
I'm making some capital white wine whey.
Will your honour be pleased to dinner to stay?"

"No, I thank you," said the fox; "but how is
poor Mrs Fox?" Then the cat answered,

"She sits all alone in her chamber upstairs,
And bewails her misfortune with floods of tears:
She weeps till her beautiful eyes are red;
For, alas! Alas! Mr Fox is dead."

"Go to her," said the other, "and say that there
is a young fox come, who wishes to marry her."

Then up went the cat, trippety trap,
And knocked at the door, tippety tap;
"Is good Mrs Fox within?" said she.
"Alas, my dear, what want you with me?"
"There waits a suitor below at the gate."

Then said Mrs Fox,

"How looks he, my dear? Is he tall and straight?
Has he nine good tails? There must be nine,
Or he never shall be a suitor of mine."

"Ah!" said the cat. "He has but one." "Then I will never have him," answered Mrs Fox.

So the cat went down, and sent this suitor about his business. Soon after, someone else knocked at the door; it was another fox that had two tails, but he was not better welcomed than the first. After this came several others, till at last one came that had really nine tails just like the old fox.

When the widow heard this, she jumped up and said,

"Now, Pussy, my dear, open windows and doors,
And bid all our friends at our wedding to meet;
And as for that nasty old master of ours,
Throw him out of the window, Puss, into the street."

But when the wedding feast was all ready, up sprang the old gentleman on a sudden, and taking a club, drove the whole company, together with Mrs Fox, out of doors.

After some time, however, the old fox really died; and soon afterwards a wolf came to pay his respects, and knocked at the door.

Wolf. "Good day, Mrs Cat, with your whiskers so trim;
How comes it you're sitting alone so prim?
What's that you are cooking so nicely, I pray?"

Cat. "O, that's bread and milk for my dinner today.
Will your worship be pleased to stay and dine,
Or shall I fetch you a glass of wine?"

"No, I thank you! Mrs Fox is not at home, I suppose?"

Cat. "She sits all alone,
Her griefs to bemoan;
For, alas! Alas! Mr Fox is gone."

Wolf. "Ah! Dear Mrs Puss! That's a loss indeed:
D'ye think she'd take *me* for a husband instead?"

Cat. "Indeed, Mr Wolf, I don't know but she may
If you'll sit down a moment, I'll step up and see."

So she gave him a chair, and shaking her ears,
She very obligingly tripped it upstairs.
She knocked at the door with the rings on her toes,
And said, "Mrs Fox, you're within, I suppose?"
"O yes," said the widow, "pray come in, my dear,
And tell me whose voice in the kitchen I hear."
"It's a wolf," said the cat, "with a nice smooth skin,

Who was passing this way, and just stepped in
To see (as old Mr Fox is dead)
If you'd like to take him for a husband instead."

"But," said Mrs Fox, "has he red feet and a sharp snout?" "No," said the cat. "Then he won't do for me." Soon after the wolf was sent about his business, there came a dog, then a goat, and after that a bear, a lion, and all the beasts, one after another. But they all wanted something that old Mr Fox had, and the cat was ordered to send them all away. At last came a young fox, and Mrs Fox said, "Has he four red feet and a sharp snout?" "Yes," said the cat.

"Then, Puss, make the parlour look clean and neat,
And throw the old gentleman into the street
A stupid old rascal! I'm glad that he's dead,
Now I've got such a charming young fox instead."

So the wedding was held, and the merry bells rung,
And the friends and relations they danced and they
   sung,
And feasted and drank, I can't tell how long.

HANSEL AND GRETTEL

HANSEL one day took his sister Grettel by the hand, and said, "Since our poor mother died we have had no happy days; for our new mother beats us all day long and when we go near her, she pushes us away. We have nothing but hard crusts to eat; and the little dog that lies by the fire is better off than we; for he sometimes has a nice piece of meat thrown to him. Heaven have mercy upon us! O if our poor mother knew how we are used! Come, we will go and travel over the wide world." They went the whole day walking over the fields, till in the evening they came to a great wood; and then they were so tired and hungry that they sat down in a hollow tree and went to sleep.

In the morning when they awoke, the sun had risen high above the trees, and shone warm upon the hollow tree. Then Hansel said, "Sister, I am very thirsty; if I could find a brook, I would go and drink, and fetch you some water too. Listen, I think I hear the sound of one." Then Hansel rose up and took Grettel by the hand and went in search of the brook. But their cruel stepmother was a fairy, and had followed them into the wood to work them mischief: and when they had found a brook that ran sparkling over the pebbles, Hansel wanted to drink; but Grettel thought she heard the brook, as it babbled along, say, "Whoever drinks here will be turned into a tiger." Then she cried out, "Ah, brother! Do not drink, or you will be turned into a wild beast and tear me to pieces." Then Hansel yielded, although he was parched with thirst. "I will wait," said he, "for the next brook." But when they came to the next, Grettel listened again, and thought she heard, "Whoever drinks here will become a wolf." Then she cried out, "Brother, brother, do not drink, or you will become a wolf and eat me." So he did not drink, but said, "I will wait for the next brook; there I must drink, say what you will, I am so thirsty."

As they came to the third brook, Grettel listened, and heard, "Whoever drinks here will become a fawn." "Ah, brother!" said she. "Do not drink, or you will be turned into a fawn and run away from me." But Hansel had already stooped down upon his knees, and the moment he put his lips into the water he was turned into a fawn.

Grettel wept bitterly over the poor creature, and the tears too rolled down his eyes as he laid himself beside her. Then she said, "Rest in peace, dear fawn, I will never leave thee." So she took off her golden necklace and put it round his neck, and plucked some rushes and plaited them into a soft string to fasten to it; and led the poor little thing by her side farther into the wood.

After they had travelled a long way, they came at last to a little cottage; and Grettel, having looked in and seen that it was quite empty, thought to herself, "We can stay and live here." Then she went and gathered leaves and moss to make a soft bed for the fawn: and every morning she went out and

She laid her head upon the fawn for a pillow

plucked nuts, roots, and berries for herself, and sweet shrubs and tender grass for her companion; and it ate out of her hand, and was pleased, and played and frisked about her. In the evening, when Grettel was tired, and had said her prayers, she laid her head upon the fawn for her pillow, and slept: and if poor Hansel could but have his right form again, they thought they should lead a very happy life.

They lived thus a long while in the wood by themselves, till it chanced that the king of that country came to hold a great hunt there. And when the fawn heard all around the echoing of the horns, and the baying of the dogs, and the merry shouts of the huntsmen, he wished very much to go and see what was going on. "Ah sister! Sister!" said he. "Let me go out into the wood, I can stay no longer." And he begged so long, that she at last agreed to let him go. "But," said she, "be sure to come to me in the evening: I shall shut up the door to keep out those wild huntsmen; but if you tap at it, and say, 'Sister, let me in,' I shall know you; but if you don't speak, I shall keep the door fast." Then away sprang the fawn, and frisked and bounded along in the open air. The king and his huntsmen saw the beautiful creature, and followed but could not overtake him; for when they thought they were sure of their prize, he sprang over the bushes and was out of sight in a moment.

As it grew dark he came running home to the hut, and tapped, and said, "Sister, sister, let me in." Then she opened the little door, and in he jumped and slept soundly all night on his soft bed.

Next morning the hunt began again; and when he heard the huntsmen's horns, he said, "Sister, open the door for me, I must go again." Then she let him out, and said, "Come back in the evening, and remember what you are to say." When the king and the huntsmen saw the fawn with the golden collar again, they gave him chase; but he was too quick for them. The chase lasted the whole day; but at last the huntsmen nearly surrounded him, and one of them wounded him in the foot, so that he became sadly lame and could hardly crawl home. The man who had wounded him followed close behind, and hid himself, and heard the little fawn say, "Sister, sister, let me in:" upon which the door opened and soon shut again. The huntsman marked all well, and went to the king and told him what he had seen and heard; then the king said, "Tomorrow we will have another chase."

Grettel was very much frightened when she saw that her dear little fawn was wounded; but she washed the blood away and put some healing herbs on it, and said, "Now go to bed, dear fawn, and you will soon be well again." The wound was so small, that in the morning there was nothing to be seen of it; and when the horn blew, the little creature said, "I can't stay here, I must go and look on; I will take care that none of them shall catch me." But Grettel said, "I am sure they will kill you this time, I will not let you go." "I shall die of vexation," answered he, "if you keep me here; when I hear the horns, I feel as if I could fly." Then Grettel was forced to let him go; so she opened the door with a heavy heart, and he bounded out gaily into the wood.

When the king saw him, he said to his huntsman, "Now chase him all day long till you catch him; but let none of you do him any harm." The sun set, however, without their being able to overtake him, and the king called away the huntsmen, and said to the one who had watched, "Now come and show me the little hut." So they went to the door and tapped, and said, "Sister, sister, let me in." Then the door opened and the king went in, and there stood a maiden more lovely than any he had ever seen. Grettel was frightened to see that it was not her fawn, but a king with a golden crown, who was come into her hut: however, he spoke kindly to her, and took her hand, and said, "Will you come with me to my castle and be my wife?" "Yes," said the maiden; "but my fawn must go with me, I cannot part with that." "Well," said the king, "he shall come and live with you all your life, and want for nothing." Just at that moment in sprang the little fawn; and his sister tied the string to his neck, and they left the hut in the wood together.

Then the king took Grettel to his palace, and celebrated the marriage in great state. And she told the king all her story; and he sent for the fairy and punished her: and the fawn was changed into Hansel again, and he and his sister loved one another, and lived happily together all their days.

THE GIANT WITH THE THREE
GOLDEN HAIRS

THERE was once a poor man who had an only son
born to him. The child was born under a lucky star;
and those who told his fortune said that in his
fourteenth year he would marry the king's daughter. It so happened that the king of that land soon
after the child's birth passed through the village in
disguise, and asked whether there was any news.
"Yes," said the people, "a child has just been born,
that they say is to be a lucky one, and when he is
fourteen years old, he is fated to marry the king's
daughter." This did not please the king; so he went
to the poor child's parents and asked them whether
they would sell him their son. "No," said they; but
the stranger begged very hard and offered a great

deal of money, and they had scarcely bread to eat, so at last they consented, thinking to themselves, he is a luck's child, he can come to no harm.

The king took the child, put it into a box, and rode away; but when he came to a deep stream, he threw it into the current, and said to himself, "That young gentleman will never be my daughter's husband." The box however floated down the stream; some kind spirit watched over it so that no water reached the child, and at last about two miles from the king's capital it stopped at the dam of a mill. The miller soon saw it, and took a long pole, and drew it towards the shore, and finding it heavy, thought there was gold inside; but when he opened it, he found a pretty little boy, who smiled upon him merrily. Now the miller and his wife had no children, and therefore rejoiced to see their prize, saying, "Heaven has sent it to us;" so they treated it very kindly, and brought it up with such care that everyone admired and loved the child.

About thirteen years passed over their heads, when the king came by accident to the mill, and asked the miller if that was his son. "No," said he, "I found him when a babe in a box in the mill dam."

"How long ago?" asked the king. "Some thirteen years," replied the miller. "He is a fine fellow," said the king. "Can you spare him to carry a letter to the queen? It will please me very much, and I will give him two pieces of gold for his trouble." "As your majesty pleases," answered the miller.

Now the king had soon guessed that this was the child whom he had tried to drown; and he wrote a letter to the queen, saying, "As soon as the bearer of this arrives let him be killed and immediately buried, so that all may be over before I return."

The young man set out with this letter, but missed his way, and came in the evening to a dark wood. Through the gloom he perceived a light at a distance, towards which he directed his course, and found that it proceeded from a little cottage. There was no one within except an old woman, who was frightened at seeing him, and said, "Why do you come hither, and whither are you going?" "I am going to the queen, to whom I was to have delivered a letter; but I have lost my way, and shall be glad if you will give me a night's rest." "You are very unlucky," said she, "for this is a robbers' hut, and if the band returns while you are here it may be worse for you." "I am so tired, however," replied he, "that I must take my chance, for I can go no farther;" so he laid the letter on the table, stretched himself out upon a bench, and fell asleep.

When the robbers came home and saw him, they asked the old woman who the strange lad was. "I have given him shelter for charity," said she; "he had a letter to carry to the queen, and lost his way." The robbers took up the letter, broke it open and read the directions which it contained to murder the bearer. Then their leader tore it, and wrote a fresh one desiring the queen, as soon as the young man arrived, to marry him to the king's daughter. Meantime they let him sleep on till morning broke, and then showed him the right way to the queen's palace; where, as soon as she had read the letter, she had all possible preparations made for the wedding; and as the young man was very beautiful, the princess took him willingly for her husband.

After a while the king returned; and when he saw the prediction fulfilled, and that this child of fortune was, notwithstanding all his cunning, married to his daughter, he inquired eagerly how this had happened, and what were the orders which he had given. "Dear husband," said the queen, "here is your letter, read it for yourself." The king took it, and seeing that an exchange had been made, asked his son-in-law what he had done with the letter which he had given him to carry. "I know nothing of it," answered he; "it must have been taken away in the night while I slept." Then the king was very wroth, and said, "No man shall have my daughter who does not descend into the wonderful cave and bring me three golden hairs from the head of the giant king who reigns there; do this and you shall have my consent." "I will soon manage that," said the youth; so he took leave of his wife and set out on his journey.

At the first city that he came to, the guard of the gate stopped him, and asked what trade he followed and what he knew. "I know everything," said he. "If that be so," replied they, "you are just the man we want; be so good as to tell us why our fountain in the marketplace is dry and will give no water; find out the cause of that, and we will give you two asses loaded with gold." "With all my heart," said he, "when I come back."

Then he journeyed on and came to another city, and there the guard also asked him what trade he followed, and what he understood. "I know everything," answered he. "Then pray do us a piece of service," said they. "Tell us why a tree which used to bear us golden apples, now does not even produce a leaf." "Most willingly," answered he, "as I come back."

At last his way led him to the side of a great lake of water over which he must pass. The ferryman soon began to ask, as the others had done, what was his trade, and what he knew. "Everything," said he. "Then," said the other, "pray inform me why I am bound for ever to ferry over this water, and have never been able to get my liberty; I will reward you handsomely." "I will tell you all about it," said the young man, "as I come home."

When he had passed the water, he came to the wonderful cave, which looked terribly black and gloomy. But the wizard king was not at home, and his grandmother sat at the door in her easy chair. "What do you seek?" said she. "Three golden hairs from the giant's head," answered he. "You run a great risk," said she, "when he returns home; yet I will try what I can do for you." Then she changed him into an ant, and told him to hide himself in the folds of her cloak. "Very well," said he: "but I want also to know why the city fountain is dry, why the tree that bore golden apples is now leafless, and what it is that binds the ferryman to his post." "Those are three puzzling questions," said the old dame; "but lie quiet and listen to what the giant says when I pull the golden hairs."

Presently night set in and the old gentleman returned home. As soon as he entered he began to snuff up the air, and cried, "All is not right here: I smell man's flesh." Then he searched all round in vain, and the old dame scolded, and said, "Why should you turn everything topsy-turvy? I have just set all in order." Upon this he laid his head in her lap and soon fell asleep. As soon as he began to snore, she seized one of the golden hairs and pulled it out. "Mercy!" cried he, starting up. "What are you about?" "I had a dream that disturbed me," said she, "and in my trouble I seized your hair; I dreamt that the fountain in the marketplace of the city was become dry and would give no water; what can be the cause?" "Ah! If they could find that out, they would be glad," said the giant: "under a stone in the fountain sits a toad; when they kill him, it will flow again."

This said, he fell asleep, and the old lady pulled out another hair. "What would you be at?" cried he in a rage. "Don't be angry," said she. "I did it in my sleep; I dreamt that in a great kingdom there was a beautiful tree that used to bear golden apples, and now has not even a leaf upon it; what is the reason of that?" "Aha!" said the giant. "They would like very well to know that secret: at the root of the tree a mouse is gnawing; if they were to kill him, the tree would bear golden apples again; if not, it will soon die. Now let me sleep in peace; if you wake me again, you shall rue it."

Then he fell once more asleep; and when she heard him snore she pulled out the third golden hair, and the giant jumped up and threatened her sorely; but she soothed him, and said, "It was a strange dream: methought I saw a ferryman who was fated to ply backwards and forwards over a lake, and could never be set at liberty; what is the charm that binds him?" "A silly fool!" said the giant. "If he were to give the rudder into the hand

She seized one of the golden hairs and pulled it out

of any passenger, he would find himself at liberty, and the other would be obliged to take his place. Now let me sleep."

In the morning the giant arose and went out; and the old woman gave the young man the three golden hairs, reminded him of the answers to his three questions, and sent him on his way.

He soon came to the ferryman, who knew him again, and asked for the answer which he had promised him. "Ferry me over first," said he, "and then I will tell you." When the boat arrived on the other side, he told him to give the rudder to any of his passengers, and then he might run away as soon as he pleased. The next place he came to was the city where the barren tree stood. "Kill the mouse," said he, "that gnaws the root, and you will have golden apples again." They gave him a rich present, and he journeyed on to the city where the fountain had dried up, and the guard demanded his answer to their question. So he told them how to cure the mischief, and they thanked him and gave him the two asses laden with gold.

And now at last this child of fortune reached home, and his wife rejoiced greatly to see him, and to hear how well everything had gone with him. He gave the three golden hairs to the king, who could no longer raise any objection to him, and when he saw all the treasure, cried out in a transport of joy, "Dear son, where did you find all this gold?" "By the side of a lake," said the youth, "where there is plenty more to be had." "Pray, tell me," said the king, "that I may go and get some too." "As much as you please," replied the other; "you will see the ferryman on the lake, let him carry you across, and there you will see gold as plentiful as sand upon the shore."

Away went the greedy king; and when he came to the lake, he beckoned to the ferryman, who took him into his boat, and as soon as he was there gave the rudder into his hand, and sprang ashore, leaving the old king to ferry away as a reward for his sins.

"And is his majesty plying there to this day?" You may be sure of that, for nobody will trouble himself to take the rudder out of his hands.

THE FROG-PRINCE

ONE fine evening a young princess went into a wood, and sat down by the side of a cool spring of water. She had a golden ball in her hand, which was her favourite plaything, and she amused herself with tossing it into the air and catching it again as it fell. After a time she threw it up so high that when she stretched out her hand to catch it, the ball bounded away and rolled along upon the ground, till at last it fell into the spring. The princess looked into the spring for her ball; but it was very deep, so deep that she could not see the bottom of it. Then she began to lament her loss, and said, "Alas! If I could only get my ball again, I would give all my fine clothes and jewels, and everything that I have in the world." Whilst she was speaking a frog put its head out of the water, and said, "Princess, why do you weep so bitterly?" "Alas!" said she. "What can you do for me, you nasty frog? My golden ball has fallen into the spring." The frog said, "I want not your pearls and jewels and fine clothes; but if you will love me and let me live with you, and eat from your little golden plate, and sleep upon your little bed, I will bring you your ball again." "What nonsense," thought the princess, "this silly frog is talking! He can never get out of the well: however, he may be able to get my ball for me; and therefore I will promise him what he asks." So she said to the frog, "Well, if you will bring me my ball, I promise to do all you require." Then the frog put his head down, and dived deep under the water; and after a little while he came up again with the ball in his mouth, and threw it on the ground. As soon as the young princess saw her ball, she ran to pick it up, and was so overjoyed to have it in her hand again, that she never thought of the frog, but ran home with it as fast as she could. The frog called after her, "Stay, princess, and take me with you as you promised;" but she did not stop to hear a word.

The next day, just as the princess had sat down to dinner, she heard a strange noise, tap-tap, as if somebody was coming up the marble staircase; and soon afterwards something knocked gently at the door, and said,

> "Open the door, my princess dear,
> Open the door to thy true love here!
> And mind the words that thou and I said,
> By the fountain cool in the greenwood shade."

Then the princess ran to the door and opened it, and there she saw the frog, whom she had quite forgotten; she was terribly frightened, and shutting the door as fast as she could, came back to her seat. The king her father asked her what had frightened her. "There is a nasty frog," said she, "at the door, who lifted my ball out of the spring this morning: I promised him that he should live with me here, thinking that he could never get out of the spring; but there he is at the door and wants to come in!"

While she was speaking the frog knocked again at the door, and said,

"Open the door, my princess dear,
Open the door to thy true love here!
And mind the words that thou and I said
By the fountain cool in the greenwood shade."

The king said to the young princess, "As you have made a promise, you must keep it; so go and let him in." She did so, and the frog hopped into the room, and came up close to the table. "Pray lift me upon a chair," said he to the princess, "and let me sit next to you." As soon as she had done this, the frog said, "Put your plate closer to me that I may eat out of it." This she did, and when he had eaten as much as he could, he said, "Now I am tired; carry me upstairs and put me into your little bed." And the princess took him up in her hand and put him upon the pillow of her own little bed, where he slept all night long. As soon as it was light he jumped up, hopped downstairs, and went out of the house. "Now," thought the princess, "he is gone, and I shall be troubled with him no more."

But she was mistaken; for when night came again, she heard the same tapping at the door, and when she opened it, the frog came in and slept upon her pillow as before till the morning broke: and the third night he did the same; but when the princess awoke on the following morning, she was astonished to see, instead of the frog, a handsome prince gazing on her with the most beautiful eyes that ever were seen, and standing at the head of her bed.

He told her that he had been enchanted by a malicious fairy, who had changed him into the form of a frog, in which he was fated to remain till some princess should take him out of the spring and let him sleep upon her bed for three nights. "You," said the prince, "have broken this cruel charm, and now I have nothing to wish for but that you should go with me into my father's kingdom, where I will marry you, and love you as long as you live."

The young princess, you may be sure, was not long in giving her consent; and as they spoke a splendid carriage drove up with eight beautiful horses decked with plumes of feathers and golden harness, and behind rode the prince's servant, the faithful Henry, who had bewailed the misfortune of his dear master so long and bitterly that his heart had well nigh burst. Then all set out full of joy for the prince's kingdom; where they arrived safely, and lived happily a great many years.

THE FOX AND THE HORSE

A FARMER had a horse that had been an excellent faithful servant to him: but he was now grown too old to work; so the farmer would give him nothing more to eat, and said, "I want you no longer, so take yourself off out of my stable; I shall not take you back again until you are stronger than a lion." Then he opened the door and turned him adrift.

The poor horse was very melancholy, and wandered up and down in the wood, seeking some little shelter from the cold wind and the rain. Presently a fox met him. "What's the matter, my friend?" said he. "Why do you hang down your head and look so lonely and woe-begone?" "Ah!" replied the horse. "Justice and avarice never dwell

in one house; my master has forgotten all that I
have done for him so many years, and because I can
no longer work he has turned me adrift, and says
unless I become stronger than a lion he will not
take me back again; what chance can I have of that?
He knows I have none, or he would not talk so."

However, the fox bid him be of good cheer,
and said, "I will help you; lie down there, stretch
yourself out quite stiff, and pretend to be dead."
The horse did as he was told, and the fox went
straight to the lion who lived in a cave close by,
and said to him, "A little way off lies a dead horse;
come with me and you may make an excellent meal
of his carcase." The lion was greatly pleased, and
set off immediately; and when they came to the
horse, the fox said, "You will not be able to eat
him comfortably here; I'll tell you what – I will tie
you fast to his tail, and then you can draw him to
your den, and eat him at your leisure."

This advice pleased the lion, so he laid himself
down quietly for the fox to make him fast to the
horse. But the fox managed to tie his legs together
and bound all so hard and fast that with all his
strength he could not set himself free. When the

work was done, the fox clapped the horse on the shoulder, and said, "Jip! Dobbin! Jip!" Then up he sprang, and moved off, dragging the lion behind him. The beast began to roar and bellow, till all the birds of the wood flew away for fright; but the horse let him sing on, and made his way quietly over the fields to his master's house.

"Here he is, master," said he, "I have got the better of him:" and when the farmer saw his old servant, his heart relented, and he said, "Thou shalt stay in thy stable and be well taken care of." And so the poor old horse had plenty to eat, and lived – till he died.

RUMPEL-STILTS-KIN

IN a certain kingdom once lived a poor miller who had a very beautiful daughter. She was moreover exceedingly shrewd and clever; and the miller was so vain and proud of her, that he one day told the king of the land that his daughter could spin gold out of straw. Now this king was very fond of money; and when he heard the miller's boast, his avarice was excited, and he ordered the girl to be brought before him. Then he led her to a chamber where there was a great quantity of straw, gave her a spinning wheel, and said, "All this must be spun into gold before morning, as you value your life." It was in vain that the poor maiden declared that she could do no such thing, the chamber was locked and she remained alone.

She sat down in one corner of the room and began to lament over her hard fate, when on a sudden the door opened, and a droll-looking little man hobbled in, and said, "Good morrow to you, my good lass, what are you weeping for?" "Alas!" answered she. "I must spin this straw into gold, and I know not how." "What will you give me," said the little man, "to do it for you?" "My necklace," replied the maiden. He took her at her word, and sat himself down to the wheel; round about it went merrily, and presently the work was done and the gold all spun.

When the king came and saw this, he was greatly astonished and pleased; but his heart grew still more greedy of gain, and he shut up the poor miller's daughter again with a fresh task. Then she knew not what to do, and sat down once more to weep; but the little man presently opened the door, and said, "What will you give me to do your task?" "The ring on my finger," replied she. So her little friend took the ring, and began to work at the wheel, till by the morning all was finished again.

The king was vastly delighted to see all this

glittering treasure; but still he was not satisfied, and took the miller's daughter into a yet larger room, and said, "All this must be spun tonight; and if you succeed, you shall be my queen." As soon as she was alone the dwarf came in, and said, "What will you give me to spin gold for you this third time?" "I have nothing left," said she. "Then promise me," said the little man, "your first little child when you are queen." "That may never be," thought the miller's daughter; and as she knew no other way to get her task done, she promised him what he asked, and he spun once more the whole heap of gold. The king came in the morning, and finding all he wanted, married her, and so the miller's daughter really became queen.

At the birth of her first little child the queen rejoiced very much, and forgot the little man and her promise; but one day he came into her chamber and reminded her of it. Then she grieved sorely at her misfortune, and offered him all the treasures of the kingdom in exchange; but in vain, till at last her tears softened him, and he said, "I will give you three days' grace, and if during that time you tell me my name you shall keep your child."

He spun once more the whole heap of gold

Now the queen lay awake all night, thinking of all the odd names that she had ever heard, and dispatched messengers all over the land to inquire after new ones. The next day the little man came, and she began with Timothy, Benjamin, Jeremiah, and all the names she could remember; but to all of them he said, "That's not my name."

The second day she began with all the comical names she could hear of, Bandy-legs, Hunch-back, Crook-shanks, and so on, but the little gentleman still said to every one of them, "That's not my name."

The third day came back one of the messengers, and said, "I can hear of no one other name; but yesterday, as I was climbing a high hill among the trees of the forest where the fox and the hare bid each other good night, I saw a little hut, and before the hut burnt a fire, and round about the fire danced a funny little man upon one leg, and sang

> "Merrily the feast I'll make,
> Today I'll brew, tomorrow bake;
> Merrily I'll dance and sing,
> For next day will a stranger bring:

      Little does my lady dream
      Rumpel-Stilts-Kin is my name!"

When the queen heard this, she jumped for joy, and as soon as her little visitor came, and said, "Now, lady, what is my name?" "Is is John?" asked she. "No!" "Is it Tom?" "No!"

      "Can your name be Rumpel-Stilts-Kin?"

"Some witch told you that! Some witch told you that!" cried the little man, and dashed his right foot in a rage so deep into the floor, that he was forced to lay hold of it with both hands to pull it out. Then he made the best of his way off, while everybody laughed at him for having had all his trouble for nothing.

THE GOOSE-GIRL

AN old queen, whose husband had been dead some years, had a beautiful daughter. When she grew up, she was betrothed to a prince who lived a great way off; and as the time drew near for her to be married, she got ready to set off on her journey to his country. Then the queen her mother packed up a great many costly things: jewels, and gold, and silver; trinkets, fine dresses, and in short everything that became a royal bride; for she loved her child very dearly: and she gave her a waiting-maid to ride with her, and give her into the bridegroom's hands; and each had a horse for the journey. Now the princess's horse was called Falada, and could speak.

When the time came for them to set out, the

old queen went into her bedchamber, and took a little knife, and cut off a lock of her hair, and gave it to her daughter, and said, "Take care of it, dear child; for it is a charm that may be of use to you on the road." Then they took a sorrowful leave of each other, and the princess put the lock of her mother's hair into her bosom, got upon her horse, and set off on her journey to her bridegroom's kingdom. One day, as they were riding along by the side of a brook, the princess began to feel very thirsty, and said to her maid, "Pray get down and fetch me some water in my golden cup out of yonder brook, for I want to drink." "Nay," said the maid, "if you are thirsty, get down yourself, and lie down by the water and drink; I shall not be your servant any longer." The princess was so thirsty that she got down, and knelt over the little brook, and drank, for she was frightened, and dared not bring out her golden cup; and then she wept, and said, "Alas! What will become of me?" And the lock of hair answered her, and said,

> "Alas! Alas! If thy mother knew it,
> Sadly, sadly she would rue it."

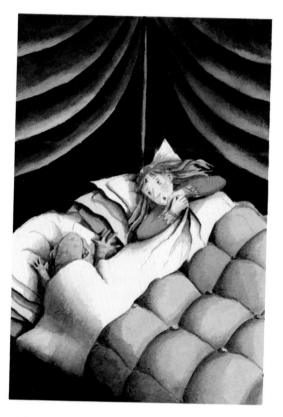

The frog slept upon her pillow (The Frog Prince)

But the princess was very humble and meek, so she said nothing to her maid's ill behaviour, but got upon her horse again.

Then all rode farther on their journey, till the day grew so warm, and the sun so scorching, that the bride began to feel very thirsty again; and at last when they came to a river she forgot her maid's rude speech, and said, "Pray get down and fetch me some water to drink in my golden cup." But the maid answered her, and even spoke more haughtily than before. "Drink if you will, but I shall not be your waiting-maid." Then the princess was so thirsty that she got off her horse, and lay down, and held her head over the running stream, and cried, and said, "What will become of me?" And the lock of hair answered her again,

> "Alas! Alas! If thy mother knew it,
> Sadly, sadly, she would rue it."

And as she leaned down to drink, the lock of hair fell from her bosom, and floated away with the river, without her seeing it, she was so frightened. But her maid saw it, and was very glad, for she knew the charm, and saw that the poor bride would be in her power, now that she had lost the hair. So when the bride would have got upon her horse again, the maid said, "I shall ride upon Falada, and you may have my horse instead:" so she was forced to give up her horse, and soon afterwards to take off her royal clothes, and put on her maid's shabby ones.

At last, as they drew near the end of their journey, this treacherous servant threatened to kill her mistress if she ever told anyone what had happened. But Falada saw it all, and marked it well. Then the waiting-maid continued upon Falada, and the real bride upon the other horse and they went on in this way till at last they came to the royal court. There was great joy at their coming, and the prince flew to meet them, and lifted the maid from her horse, thinking she was the one who was to be his wife; and she was led upstairs to the royal chamber, while the true princess was told to stay in the court below.

But the old king happened to be looking out of the window, and saw her in the yard below; and as she looked very pretty, and too delicate for a waiting-maid, he went into the royal chamber to ask the bride who it was she had brought with her, that was thus left standing in the court below. "I brought her with me for the sake of her company on the road," said she; "pray give the girl some work to do, that she may not be idle." The old king could not for some time think of any work for her to do; but at last he said, "I have a lad who takes care of my geese; she may go and help him." Now the name of this lad, that the real bride was to help in watching the king's geese, was Curdken.

Soon after, the false bride said to the prince, "Dear husband, pray do me one piece of kindness." "That I will," said the prince. "Then tell one of your slaughterers to cut off the head of the horse I rode upon, for it was very unruly, and plagued me sadly on the road:" but the truth was, she was very much afraid lest Falada should speak, and tell all she had done to the princess. She carried her point, and the faithful Falada was killed: but when the true princess heard of it, she wept, and begged the man to nail up Falada's head against a large dark gate of the city, through which she had to pass every morning and evening, that there she might still see him sometimes. Then the slaughterer said he would

do as she wished; and cut off the head, and nailed it
fast under the dark gate.

Early the next morning, as she and Curdken
went out through the gate, she said sorrowfully,

> "Falada, Falada, there thou art hanging!"

and the head answered,

> "Bride, bride, there thou art ganging!
> Alas! Alas! If thy mother knew it,
> Sadly, sadly her heart would rue it."

Then they went out of the city, and drove
the geese on to the green meadow. There she sat
down upon a bank and let down her waving locks
of hair, which were as fair as silver; and when
Curdken saw it glitter in the sun, he ran up, and
would have pulled some of the locks out; but she
cried,

> "Blow, breezes, blow!
> Let Curdken's hat go!
> Blow, breezes, blow!
> Let him after it go!
> O'er hills, dales, and rocks,

Away be it whirled,
Till the silvery locks
Are all combed and curled!"

Then there came a wind, so strong that it blew off Curdken's hat; and away it flew over the hills, and he after it; till, by the time he came back, she had done combing her hair, and put it up under her kerchief. Then he was very angry and sulky, and would not speak to her at all; but they watched the geese until it grew dark in the evening, and then drove them homewards.

The next morning, as they were going through the dark gate, the poor girl looked up at Falada's head, and cried,

"Falada, Falada, there thou art hanging!"

and it answered,

"Bride, bride, there thou art ganging!
Alas! Alas! If thy mother knew it,
Sadly, sadly her heart would rue it."

Then she drove on the geese, and sat down again in the meadow, and began to comb out her hair as before; and Curdken ran up to her, and wanted to take hold of it; but she cried out quickly,

"Blow, breezes, blow!
Let Curdken's hat go!
Blow, breezes, blow!
Let him after it go!
O'er hills, dales, and rocks,
Away be it whirled,
Till the silvery locks
Are all combed and curled!"

Then the wind came and blew his hat, and off it flew a great way, over the hills and far away, so that he had to run after it; and when he came back, she had done up her hair again, and all was safe. So they watched the geese till it grew dark.

In the evening, after they came home, Curdken went to the old king, and said, "I cannot have that strange girl to help me to keep the geese any longer." "Why?" said the king. "Because she does nothing but tease me all day long." Then the king made him tell him all that had passed. And Curdken said, "When we go in the morning through the dark gate with our flock of geese, she weeps, and talks with the head of a horse that hangs upon the wall, and says,

"Falada, Falada, there thou art hanging!"

and the head answers,

"Bride, bride, there thou art ganging!
Alas! Alas! If thy mother knew it,
Sadly, sadly her heart would rue it."

And Curdken went on telling the king what had happened upon the meadow where the geese fed; and how his hat was blown away, and he was forced to run after it, and leave his flock. But the old king told him to go out again as usual the next day; and when morning came, he placed himself behind the dark gate, and heard how she spoke to Falada, and how Falada answered; and then he went into the field, and hid himself in a bush by the meadow's side, and soon saw with his own eyes how they drove the flock of geese, and how, after a little time, she let down her hair that glittered in the sun; and then he heard her say,

> "Blow, breezes blow!
> Let Curdken's hat go!
> Blow, breezes, blow!
> Let him after it go!
> O'er hills, dales, and rocks,
> Away be it whirled,
> Till the silvery locks
> Are all combed and curled!"

And soon came a gale of wind, and carried away Curdken's hat, while the girl went on combing and curling her hair. All this the old king saw: so he went home without being seen; and when the little goose-girl came back in the evening, he called her aside, and asked her why she did so; but she burst into tears, and said, "That I must not tell you or any man, or I shall lose my life."

But the old king begged so hard, that she had no peace till she had told him all, word for word: and it was very lucky for her that she did so, for the king ordered royal clothes to be put upon her, and gazed on her with wonder she was so beautiful. Then he called his son, and told him that he had only the false bride, for that she was merely a waiting-maid, while the true one stood by. And the young king rejoiced when he saw her beauty, and heard how meek and patient she had been; and, without saying anything, ordered a great feast to be got ready for all his court. The bridegroom sat at the top, with the false princess on one side, and the true one on the other; but nobody knew her, for she was quite dazzling to their eyes, and was not at all like the little goose-girl, now that she had her brilliant dress.

When they had eaten and drunk, and were very merry, the old king told all the story, as one that he had once heard of, and asked the one-time waiting-maid what she thought ought to be done to anyone who would behave thus. "Nothing better," said this false bride, "than that she should be thrown into a cask stuck round with sharp nails, and that two white horses should be put to it, and should drag it from street to street till she is dead." "Thou art she!" said the old king. "And since thou hast judged thyself, it shall be so done to thee." And the young king was married to his true wife, and they reigned over the kingdom in peace and happiness all their lives.

ASHPUTTEL

THE wife of a rich man fell sick: and when she felt that her end drew nigh, she called her only daughter to her bedside, and said, "Always be a good girl, and I will look down from heaven and watch over you." Soon afterwards she shut her eyes and died, and was buried in the garden; and the little girl went every day to her grave and wept, and was always good and kind to all about her. And the snow spread a beautiful white covering over the grave; but by the time the sun had melted it away again, her father had married another wife. This new wife had two daughters of her own, that she brought home with her: they were fair in face, but foul at heart, and it was now a sorry time for the poor little girl. "What does the good-for-nothing thing want in the parlour?" said they. "They who would eat bread should first earn it; away with the kitchen maid!" Then they took away her fine clothes, and gave her an old grey frock to put on, and laughed at her and shoved her into the kitchen.

There she was forced to do hard work; to rise early before daylight, to bring the water, to make the fire, to cook and to wash. Besides that, the sisters plagued her in all sorts of ways and laughed at her. In the evening when she was tired she had no bed to lie down on, but was made to lie by the hearth among the ashes; and then, as she was of course always dusty and dirty, they called her Ashputtel.

It happened once that the father was going to the fair, and asked his wife's daughters what he should bring them. "Fine clothes," said the first. "Pearls and diamonds," cried the second. "Now, child," said he to his own daughter, "what will you have?" "The first sprig, dear father, that rubs against your hat on your way home," said she. Then he bought for the two first the fine clothes and pearls and diamonds they had asked for: and on his way

home as he rode through a green copse, a sprig of
hazel brushed against him, and almost pushed off
his hat: so he broke it off and brought it away; and
when he got home he gave it to his daughter. Then
she took it and went to her mother's grave and
planted it there, and cried so much that it was
watered with her tears; and there it grew and
became a fine tree. Three times every day she went
to it and wept; and soon a little bird came and built
its nest upon the tree, and talked with her, and
watched over her, and brought her whatever she
wished for.

Now it happened that the king of the land held
a feast which was to last three days, and out of
those who came to it his son was to choose a bride
for himself: and Ashputtel's two sisters were asked
to come. So they called her up, and said, "Now,
comb our hair, brush our shoes, and tie our sashes
for us, for we are going to dance at the king's
feast." Then she did as she was told, but when all
was done she could not help crying, for she thought
to herself, she should have liked to go to the dance
too; and at last she begged her mother very hard to
let her go. "You! Ashputtel?" she said. "You who

have nothing to wear, no clothes at all, and who cannot even dance – you want to go to the ball?" And when she kept on begging, to get rid of her, she said at last, "I will throw this basinful of peas into the ash heap, and if you have picked them all out in two hours' time you shall go to the feast too." Then she threw the peas into the ashes: but the little maiden ran out at the back door into the garden, and cried out,

> "Hither, hither, through the sky,
> Turtle-doves and linnets, fly!
> Blackbird, thrush, and chaffinch gay,
> Hither, hither, haste away!
> One and all, come help me quick,
> Haste ye, haste ye, pick, pick pick!"

Then first came two white doves flying in at the kitchen window; and next came two turtle-doves; and after them all the little birds under heaven came chirping and fluttering in, and flew down into the ashes: and the little doves stooped their heads down and set to work, pick, pick, pick; and then the others began to pick, pick, pick; and picked out all the good grain and put it in a dish,

and left the ashes. At the end of one hour the work
was done, and all flew out again at the windows.
Then she brought the dish to her mother, overjoyed
at the thought that now she should go to the feast.
But she said, "No, no! You slut, you have no
clothes and cannot dance, you shall not go." And
when Ashputtel begged very hard to go, she said,
"If you can in one hour's time pick two of those
dishes of peas out of the ashes, you shall go too."
And thus she thought she should at last get rid of
her. So she shook two dishes of peas into the ashes;
but the little maiden went out into the garden at the
back of the house, and cried out as before,

> 'Hither, hither, through the sky,
> Turtle-doves and linnets, fly!
> Blackbird, thrush, and chaffinch gay,
> Hither, hither, haste away!
> One and all, come help me quick,
> Haste ye, haste ye, pick, pick, pick!"

Then first came two white doves in at the
kitchen window; and next came the turtle-doves;
and after them all the little birds under heaven came
chirping and hopping about, and flew down about

the ashes: and the little doves put their heads down
and set to work, pick, pick, pick; and then the
others began to pick, pick, pick; and they put all
the good grain into the dishes, and left all the ashes.
Before half an hour's time all was done, and out
they flew again. And then Ashputtel took the dishes
to her mother, rejoicing to think that she should
now go to the ball. But her mother said, "It is all
of no use, you cannot go; you have no clothes, and
cannot dance, and you would only put us to
shame:" and off she went with her two daughters
to the feast.

Now when all were gone, and nobody left at
home, Ashputtel went sorrowfully and sat down
under the hazel tree, and cried out,

> "Shake, shake, hazel tree,
> Gold and silver over me!"

Then her friend the bird flew out of the tree
and brought a gold and silver dress for her, and
slippers of spangled silk: and she put them on, and
followed her sisters to the feast. But they did not
know her, and thought it must be some strange
princess, she looked so fine and beautiful in her rich

clothes; and they never once thought of Ashputtel, but took for granted that she was safe at home in the dirt.

The king's son soon came up to her, and took her by the hand and danced with her and no one else: and he never left her hand; but when anyone else came to ask her to dance, he said, "This lady is dancing with me." Thus they danced till a late hour of the night; and then she wanted to go home: and the king's son said, "I shall go and take care of you to your home;" for he wanted to see where the beautiful maid lived. But she slipped away from him unawares, and ran off towards home, and the prince followed her; but she jumped up into the pigeon house and shut the door. Then he waited till her father came home, and told him that the unknown maiden who had been at the feast had hid herself in the pigeon house. But when they had broken open the door they found no one within; and as they came back into the house, Ashputtel lay, as she always did, in her dirty frock by the ashes, and her dim little lamp burnt in the chimney: for she had run as quickly as she could through the pigeon house and on to the hazel tree, and had there

There came a wind so strong that it blew off Curdken's hat
(The Goose-Girl)

taken off her beautiful clothes, and laid them beneath the tree, that the bird might carry them away, and had seated herself amid the ashes again in her little grey frock.

The next day when the feast was again held, and her father, mother, and sisters were gone, Ashputtel went to the hazel tree, and said,

> "Shake, shake, hazel tree,
> Gold and silver over me!"

And the bird came and brought a still finer dress than the one she had worn the day before. And when she came in it to the ball, everyone wondered at her beauty: but the king's son, who was waiting for her, took her by the hand, and danced with her; and when anyone asked her to dance, he said as before, "This lady is dancing with me." When night came she wanted to go home; and the king's son followed her as before, that he might see into what house she went: but she sprang away from him all at once into the garden behind her father's house. In this garden stood a fine large pear tree full of ripe fruit; and Ashputtel not knowing where to hide herself jumped up into it without

being seen. Then the king's son could not find out
where she was gone, but waited till her father came
home, and said to him, "The unknown lady who
danced with me has slipped away, and I think she
must have sprung into the pear tree." The father
thought to himself, "Can it be Ashputtel?" So he
ordered an axe to be brought; and they cut down
the tree, but found no one upon it. And when they
came back into the kitchen, there lay Ashputtel in
the ashes as usual; for she had slipped down on the
other side of the tree, and carried her beautiful
clothes back to the bird at the hazel tree, and then
put on her little grey frock.

The third day, when her father and mother and
sisters were gone, she went again into the garden,
and said,

> "Shake, shake, hazel tree,
> Gold and silver over me!"

Then her kind friend the bird brought a dress
still finer than the former one, and slippers which
were all of gold: so that when she came to the feast
no one knew what to say for wonder at her beauty:
and the king's son danced with her alone; and when

anyone else asked her to dance, he said, "This lady is my partner." Now when night came she wanted to go home; and the king's son would go with her, and said to himself, "I will not lose her this time;" but however she managed to slip away from him, though in such a hurry that she dropped her left golden slipper upon the stairs.

So the prince took the shoe, and went the next day to the king his father, and said, "I will take for my wife the lady that this golden slipper fits." Then both the sisters were overjoyed to hear this; for they had beautiful feet, and had no doubt that they could wear the golden slipper. The eldest went first into the room where the slipper was and wanted to try it on, and the mother stood by. But her great toe could not go into it, and the shoe was altogether much too small for her. Then the mother gave her a knife, and said, "Never mind, cut it off; when you are queen you will not care about toes, you will not want to go on foot." So the silly girl cut her great toe off, and squeezed the shoe on, and went to the king's son. Then he took her for his bride, and set her beside him on his horse and rode away with her.

But on their way home they had to pass by the hazel tree that Ashputtel had planted, and there sat a little dove on the branch singing,

"Back again! Back again! Look to the shoe!
The shoe is too small, and not made for you!
Prince! Prince! look again for thy bride,
For she's not the true one that sits by thy side."

Then the prince got down and looked at her foot, and saw by the blood that streamed from it what a trick she had played him. So he turned his horse round and brought the false bride back to her home, and said, "This is not the right bride; let the other sister try and put on the slipper." Then she went into the room and got her foot into the shoe, all but the heel, which was too large. But her mother squeezed it in till the blood came, and took her to the king's son; and he set her as his bride by his side on his horse, and rode away with her.

But when they came to the hazel tree the little dove sat there still, and sang,

"Back again! Back again! Look to the shoe!
The shoe is too small, and not made for you!

Prince! Prince! Look again for thy bride,
For she's not the true one that sits by thy side."

Then he looked down and saw that the blood
streamed so from the shoe that her white stockings were quite red. So he turned his horse and
brought her back again also. "This is not the true
bride," said he to the father; "have you no other
daughters?" "No," said he; "there is only a little
dirty Ashputtel here, the child of my first wife; I
am sure she cannot be the bride." However, the
prince told him to send her. But the mother said,
"No, no, she is much too dirty, she will not dare
to show herself:" however, the prince would have
her come. And she first washed her face and
hands, and then went in and curtsied to him, and
he reached her the golden slipper. Then she took
her clumsy shoe off her left foot, and put on the
golden slipper; and it fitted her as if it had been
made for her. And when he drew near and looked
at her face he knew her, and said, "This is the right
bride." But the mother and both the sisters were
frightened and turned pale with anger as he took
Ashputtel on his horse, and rode away with her.

And when they came to the hazel tree, the white dove sang,

> "Home! Home! Look at the shoe!
> Princess! The shoe was made for you!
> Prince! Prince! Take home thy bride,
> For she is the true one that sits by thy side!"

And when the dove had done its song, it came flying and perched upon her right shoulder, and so went home with her.

CHERRY, OR THE FROG-BRIDE

THERE was once a king who had three sons. Not far from his kingdom lived an old woman who had an only daughter called Cherry. The king sent his sons out to see the world, that they might learn the ways of foreign lands, and get wisdom and skill in ruling the kingdom that they were one day to have for their own. But the old woman lived at peace at home with her daughter, who was called Cherry, because she liked cherries better than any other kind of food, and would eat scarcely anything else. Now her poor old mother had no garden, and no money to buy cherries every day for her daughter; and at last there was no other plan left but to go to a neighbouring nunnery-garden and beg the finest she could get of the nuns; for she dared not let her daughter go out by herself, as she was very pretty, and she feared some mischance might befall her. Cherry's taste was, however, very well known; and as it happened that the abbess was as fond of cherries as she was, it was soon found out where all the best fruit went; and the holy mother was not a little angry at missing some of her stock and finding whither it had gone.

The princes while wandering on came one day to the town where Cherry and her mother lived; and as they passed along the street saw the fair maiden standing at the window, combing her long and beautiful locks of hair. Then each of the three fell deeply in love with her, and began to say how much he longed to have her for his wife! Scarcely had the wish been spoken, when all drew their swords, and a dreadful battle began; the fight lasted long, and their rage grew hotter and hotter, when at last the abbess hearing the uproar came to the gate. Finding that her neighbour was the cause, her old spite against her broke forth at once, and in her rage she wished Cherry turned into an ugly frog, and sitting in the water under the bridge at the world's end. No sooner said than done; and poor Cherry became a frog, and vanished out of their sight. The princes had now nothing to fight for; so sheathing their swords again, they shook hands as brothers, and went on towards their father's home.

The old king meanwhile found that he grew weak and ill-fitted for the business of reigning: so he thought of giving up his kingdom; but to whom should it be? This was a point that his fatherly heart could not settle; for he loved all his sons alike. "My dear children," said he, "I grow old and weak, and should like to give up my kingdom; but I cannot make up my mind which of you to choose for my heir, for I love you all three; and besides, I should wish to give my people the cleverest and best of you for their king. However, I will give you three trials, and the one who wins the prize shall have the kingdom. The first is to seek me out one hundred ells of cloth, so fine that I can draw it through my golden ring." The sons said they would do their best, and set out on the search.

The two eldest brothers took with them many followers, and coaches and horses of all sorts, to bring home all the beautiful cloth which they should find; but the youngest went alone by himself. A point came where the roads branched off into several ways; two ran through smiling meadows, with smooth paths and shady groves, but the third looked dreary and dirty, and went over barren wastes. The two eldest chose the pleasant ways; and the youngest took his leave and whistled along over the dreary road. Whenever fine linen was to be seen, the two elder brothers bought it, and bought so much that their coaches and horses bent under their burden. The younger, on the other hand, journeyed on many a weary day, and found not a place where he could buy even one piece of cloth that was at all fine and good. His heart sank beneath him, and every mile he grew more and more heavy and sorrowful. At last he came to a bridge over a stream, and there he sat himself down to rest and sigh over his bad luck, when an ugly-looking frog popped its head out of the water, and asked, with a voice that had not at all a harsh sound to his ears, what was the matter. The prince said in a pet, "Silly frog! Thou canst not help me." "Who told you so?" said the frog. "Tell me what ails you." After a while the prince opened

the whole story, and told why his father had sent
him out. "I will help you," said the frog; so it
jumped back into the stream and soon came back
dragging a small piece of linen not bigger than
one's hand, and by no means the cleanest in the
world in its look. However, there it was, and the
prince was told to take it away with him. He had
no great liking for such a dirty rag; but still there
was something in the frog's speech that pleased him
much, and he thought to himself, "It can do no
harm, it is better than nothing"; so he picked it up,
put it in his pocket, and thanked the frog, who
dived down again, panting and quite tired, as it
seemed, with its work. To his great joy, the farther
he went the heavier he found the pocket grow, and
so he turned himself homewards, trusting greatly
in his good luck.

He reached home nearly about the same time
that his brothers came up, with their horses and
coaches all heavily laden. Then the old king was
very glad to see his children again, and pulled the
ring off his finger to try who had done the best; but
in all the stock which the two eldest had brought
there was not one piece a tenth part of which would

go through the ring. At this they were greatly
abashed; for they had made a laugh of their brother,
who came home, as they thought, empty-handed.
But how great was their anger, when they saw him
pull from his pocket a piece that for softness,
beauty, and whiteness, was a thousand times better
than anything that was ever before seen! It was so
.fine that it passed with ease through the ring;
indeed, two such pieces would readily have gone in
together. The father embraced the lucky youth,
told his servants to throw the coarse linen into the
sea, and said to his children, "Now you must set
about the second task which I am to set you; bring
me home a little dog, so small that it will lie in a
nutshell."

His sons were not a little frightened at such a
task; but they all longed for the crown, and made
up their minds to go and try their hands, and so
after a few days they set out once more on their
travels. At the crossways they parted as before, and
the youngest chose his old dreary rugged road with
all the bright hopes that his former good luck gave
him. Scarcely had he sat himself down again at the
bridge foot, when his old friend the frog jumped

out, set itself beside him, and as before opened its big wide mouth, and croaked out, "What is the matter?" The prince had this time no doubt of the frog's power, and therefore told what he wanted. "It shall be done for you," said the frog; and springing into the stream it soon brought up a hazelnut, laid it at his feet, and told him to take it home to his father, and crack it gently, and then see what would happen. The prince went his way very well pleased, and the frog, tired with its task, jumped back into the water.

His brothers had reached home first, and brought with them a great many very pretty little dogs. The old king, willing to help them all he could, sent for a large walnut-shell and tried it with every one of the little dogs; but one stuck fast with the hindfoot out, and another with the head, and a third with the forefoot, and a fourth with its tail, in short, some one way and some another; but none was at all likely to sit easily in this new kind of kennel. When all had been tried, the youngest made his father a dutiful bow, and gave him the hazelnut, begging him to crack it very carefully: the moment this was done out ran a beautiful little white dog upon the king's hand, wagged its tail, fondled his new master, and soon turned about and barked at the other little beasts in the most graceful manner, to the delight of the whole court. The joy of everyone was great; the old king again embraced his lucky son, told his people to drown all the other dogs in the sea, and said to his children, "Dear sons! Your weightiest tasks are now over; listen to my last wish; whoever brings home the fairest lady shall be at once the heir to my crown."

The prize was so tempting and the chance so fair for all, that none made any doubts about setting to work, each in his own way, to try and be the winner. The youngest was not in such good spirits as he was the last time; he thought to himself, "The old frog has been able to do a great deal for me; but all its power must be nothing to me now, for where should it find me a fair maiden, still less a fairer maiden than was ever seen at my father's court? The swamps where it lives have no living things in them, but toads, snakes, and such vermin." Meantime he went on, and sighed as he sat down again with a heavy heart by the bridge. "Ah frog!" said he. "This time thou canst do me no good." "Never mind," croaked the frog: "only tell me what is the matter now." Then the prince told his old friend what trouble had now come upon him. "Go thy ways home," said the frog; "the fair maiden will follow hard after; but take care and do not laugh at whatever may happen!" This said, it sprang as before into the water and was soon out of sight. The prince still sighed on, for he trusted very little this time to the frog's word; but he had not set many steps towards home before he heard a noise behind him, and looking round saw six large water rats dragging along a large pumpkin like a coach, full trot. On the box sat an old fat toad as coachman, and behind stood two little frogs as footmen, and two fine mice with stately whiskers ran before as outriders; within sat his old friend the frog, rather misshapen and unseemly to be sure, but still with somewhat of a graceful air as it bowed to him in passing. Much too deeply wrapped in thought as to his chance of finding the fair lady whom he was seeking, to take any heed of the strange scene before him, the prince scarcely looked at it, and had still less mind to laugh. The coach passed on a little way, and soon turned a corner that hid it from his sight; but how astonished was he, on turning the corner himself, to find a handsome coach and six black horses standing there, with a coachman in gay livery, and within, the most beautiful lady he had ever seen, whom he soon knew to be the fair Cherry, for whom his heart had so long ago panted! As he came up, the servants opened the coach door, and he was allowed to seat himself by the beautiful lady.

They soon came to his father's city, where his brothers also came, with trains of fair ladies; but as soon as Cherry was seen, all the court gave her with one voice the crown of beauty. The delighted father embraced his son, and named him the heir to his crown, and ordered all the other ladies to be thrown like the little dogs into the sea and drowned. Then the prince married Cherry, and lived long and happily with her, and indeed lives with her still – if he be not dead.

MOTHER HOLLE

A widow had two daughters; one of them was very pretty and thrifty, but the other was ugly and idle.

Odd as you may think it, she loved the ugly and idle one much the best, and the other was made to do all the work, and was in short quite the drudge of the whole house. Every day she had to sit on a bench by a well on the side of the high road before the house, and spin so much that her fingers were quite sore, and at length the blood would come. Now it happened that once when her fingers had bled and the spindle was all bloody, she dipped it into the well, and meant to wash it, but unluckily it fell from her hand and dropped in. Then she ran crying to her mother, and told her what had happened; but she scolded her sharply, and said, "If you have been so silly as to let the spindle fall in, you must get it out again as well as you can." So the poor little girl went back to the well, and knew not how to begin, but in her sorrow threw herself into the water, and sank down to the bottom senseless. In a short time she seemed to awake as from a trance, and came to herself again; and when she opened her eyes and looked around, she saw she was in a beautiful meadow, where the sun shone brightly, the birds sang sweetly on the boughs, and thousands of flowers sprang beneath her feet.

Then she rose up, and walked along this delightful meadow, and came to a pretty cottage by the side of a wood; and when she went in she saw an oven full of new bread baking, and the bread said, "Pull me out! Pull me out or I shall be burnt, for I am quite done enough." So she stepped up quickly and took it all out. Then she went on farther, and came to a tree that was full of fine rosy-cheeked apples, and it said to her, "Shake me! Shake me! We are all quite ripe!" So she shook the tree, and the apples fell down like a shower, until there were no more upon the tree. Then she went on again, and at length came to a small cottage where an old woman was sitting at the door: the little girl would have run away, but the old woman called out after her, "Don't be frightened, my dear child! Stay with me, I should like to have you for my little maid, and if you do all the work in the house neatly you shall fare well; but take care to make my bed nicely, and shake it every morning out at the door, so that the feathers may fly, for then the good people below say it snows. I am Mother Holle."

As the old woman spoke so kindly to her, the girl was willing to do as she said; so she went into her employ, and took care to do everything to please her, and always shook the bed well, so that she led a very quiet life with her, and every day had good meat both boiled and roast to eat for her dinner.

But when she had been some time with the old lady, she became sorrowful, and although she was much better off here than at home, still she had a longing towards it, and at length said to her mistress, "I used to grieve at my troubles at home, but if they were all to come again, and I were sure of faring ever so well here, I could not stay any longer." "You are right," said her mistress. "You shall do as you like; and as you have worked for me so faithfully, I will myself show you the way back again." Then she took her by the hand and led her behind her cottage, and opened a door, and as the girl stood underneath there fell a heavy shower of gold, so that she held out her apron and caught a great deal of it. And the fairy put a shining golden dress over her, and said, "All this you shall have because you have behaved so well;" and she gave her back the spindle too which had fallen into the well, and led her out by another door. When it shut behind her, she found herself not far from her mother's house; and as she went into the courtyard the cock sat upon the well head and clapped his wings and cried out,

> "Cock-a-doodle-doo!
> Our golden lady's come home again."

Then she went into the house, and as she was so rich she was welcomed home. When her mother heard how she got these riches, she wanted to have the same luck for her ugly and idle daughter, so she too was told to sit by the well and spin. That her spindle might be bloody, she pricked her fingers with it, and when that would not do she thrust her hand into a thornbush. Then she threw it into the well and sprang in herself after it. Like her sister, she came to a beautiful meadow, and followed the same path. When she came to the oven in the cottage, the bread called out as before, "Take me out! Or I shall burn, I am quite done enough." But the lazy girl said, "A pretty story, indeed! Just as if I should dirty myself for you!" and went on her way. She soon came to the apple tree that cried, "Shake me! Shake me! For my apples are quite ripe!" but she answered, "I will take care how I do that, for one of you might fall upon my head;" so she went on. At length she came to Mother Holle's house, and readily agreed to be her maid. The first day she behaved herself very well, and did what her mistress told her; for she thought of the gold she would give her; but the second day she began to be lazy, and the third still more so, for she would not get up in the morning early enough, and when she did she made the bed very badly, and did not shake it so that the feathers would fly out. Mother Holle was soon tired of her, and turned her off; but the lazy girl was quite pleased at that, and thought to herself, "Now the golden rain will come." Then the fairy took her to the same door; but when she stood under it, instead of gold a great kettle full of dirty pitch came showering upon her. "That is your wages," said Mother Holle as she shut the door upon her. So she went home quite black with the pitch, and as she came near her mother's house the cock sat upon the well, and clapped his wings, and cried out,

> "Cock-a-doodle-doo!
> Our dirty slut's come home again!"

THE WATER OF LIFE

LONG before you and I were born there reigned, in a country a great way off, a king who had three sons. This king once fell very ill, so ill that nobody thought he would live. His sons were very much grieved at their father's sickness; and as they walked weeping in the garden of the palace, an old man met them and asked what they ailed. They told him their father was so ill that they were afraid nothing could save him. "I know what would," said the old man. "It is the Water of Life. If he could have a draught of it he would be well again, but it is very hard to get." Then the eldest son said, "I will soon find it," and went to the sick king, and begged that he might go in search of the Water of Life, as it was the only thing that could save him. "No," said the king; "I had rather die than place you in such great danger as you must meet with in your journey." But he begged so hard that the king let him go; and the prince thought to himself, "If I bring my father this water I shall be his dearest son, and he will make me heir to his kingdom."

Then he set out, and when he had gone on his way some time he came to a deep valley overhung with rocks and woods; and as he looked around there stood above him on one of the rocks a little dwarf, who called out to him and said, "Prince, whither hastest thou so fast?" "What is that to you, little ugly one?" said the prince sneeringly, and rode on his way. But the little dwarf fell into a great rage at his behaviour, and laid a spell of ill luck upon him, so that, as he rode on, the mountain pass seemed to become narrower and narrower, and at last the way was so straitened that he could not go a step forward, and when he thought to have turned his horse round and gone back the way he came, the passage he found had closed behind also, and shut him quite up; he next tried to get off his horse and make his way on foot, but this he was unable to do, and so there he was forced to abide spellbound.

Meantime the king his father was lingering on in daily hope of his return, till at last the second son said, "Father, I will go in search of this Water;" for he thought to himself, "My brother is surely dead, and the kingdom will fall to me if I have good luck in my journey." The king was at first very unwilling to let him go, but at last yielded to his wish. So he set out and followed the same road which his brother had taken, and met the same dwarf, who stopped him at the same spot, and said as before, "Prince, whither hastest thou so fast?" "Mind your own affairs, busybody!" answered the prince scornfully, and rode off. But the dwarf put the same enchantment upon him, and when he came like the other to the narrow pass in the mountains he could neither move forward nor backward. Thus it is with proud silly people, who think themselves too wise to take advice.

When the second prince had thus stayed away a long while, the youngest said he would go and search for the Water of Life, and trusted he should soon be able to make his father well again. The dwarf met him too at the same spot, and said, "Prince, whither hastest thou so fast?" and the prince said, "I go in search of the Water of Life, because my father is ill and like to die: can you help me?" "Do you know where it is to be found?" asked the dwarf. "No," said the prince. "Then as you have spoken to me kindly and sought for advice, I will tell you how and where to go. The Water you seek springs from a well in an enchanted castle, and that you may be able to go in safety I will give you an iron wand and two little loaves of bread; strike the iron door of the castle three times with the wand, and it will open: two hungry lions will be lying down inside gaping for their prey; but if you throw them the bread they will let you pass; then hasten on to the well and take some of the Water of Life before the clock strikes twelve, for if you tarry longer the door will shut upon you for ever."

Then the prince thanked the dwarf for his friendly aid, and took the wand and the bread and went travelling on and on over sea and land, till he came to his journey's end, and found everything to be as the dwarf had told him. The door flew open at the third stroke of the wand, and when the lions were quieted he went on through the castle, and came at length to a beautiful hall; around it he saw several knights sitting in a trance; then he pulled off their rings and put them on his own fingers. In another room he saw on a table a sword and a loaf of bread, which he also took. Farther on he came to a room where a beautiful young lady sat upon a couch, who welcomed him joyfully, and said, if he would set her free from the spell that bound her, the kingdom should be his if he would come back in a year and marry her; then she told him that the well that held the Water of Life was in the palace gardens, and bade him make haste and draw what he wanted before the clock struck twelve. Then he went on, and as he walked through beautiful gardens he came to a delightful shady spot in which stood a couch; and he thought to himself, as he felt tired, that he would rest himself for a while and gaze on the lovely scenes around him. So he laid himself down, and sleep fell upon him unawares and he did not wake up till the clock was striking a quarter to twelve; then he sprang from the couch dreadfully frightened, ran to the well, filled a cup that was standing by him full of Water, and hastened to get away in time. Just as he was going out of the iron door it struck twelve, and the door fell so quickly upon him that it tore away a piece of his heel.

When he found himself safe he was overjoyed to think that he had got the water of Life; and as he was going on his way homewards, he passed by the little dwarf, who when he saw the sword and the loaf said, "You have made a noble prize; with the sword you can at a blow slay whole armies, and the bread will never fail." Then the prince thought to himself, "I cannot go home to my father without my brothers;" so he said, "Dear dwarf, cannot you tell me where my two brothers are, who set out in search of the Water of Life before me and never came back?" "I have shut them up by a charm between two mountains," said the dwarf, "because they were proud and ill-behaved, and scorned to ask advice." The prince begged so hard for his brothers that the dwarf at last set them free, though unwillingly saying, "Beware of them, for they have bad hearts." Their brother, however, was greatly rejoiced to see them, and told them all that had happened to him, how he had found the Water of

Life, and had taken a cupful of it, and how he had set a beautiful princess free from a spell that bound her; and how she had engaged to wait a whole year, and then to marry him and give him the kingdom. Then they all three rode on together, and on their way home came to a country that was laid waste by war and a dreadful famine, so that it was feared all must die for want. But the prince gave the king of the land the bread, and all his kingdom ate of it. And he slew the enemy's army with the wonderful sword, and left the kingdom in peace and plenty. In the same manner he befriended two other countries that they passed through on their way.

When they came to the sea, they got into a ship, and during their voyage the two eldest said to themselves, "Our brother has got the Water which we could not find, therefore our father will forsake us, and give him the kingdom which is our right;" so they were full of envy and revenge, and agreed together how they could ruin him. They waited till he was fast asleep, and then poured the Water of Life out of the cup and took it for themselves, giving him bitter sea water instead. And when they came to their journey's end, the youngest son brought his cup to the sick king, that he might drink and be healed. Scarcely, however, had he tasted the bitter sea water when he became worse even than he was before, and then both the elder sons came in and blamed the youngest for what he had done, and said that he wanted to poison their father, but that they had found the Water of Life and had brought it with them. He no sooner began to drink of what they brought him, than he felt his sickness leave him, and was as strong and well as in his young days; then they went to their brother and laughed at him, and said, "Well, brother, you found the Water of Life, did you? You have had the trouble and we shall have the reward; pray, with all your cleverness why did not you manage to keep your eyes open? Next year one of us will take away your beautiful princess, if you do not take care; you had better say nothing about this to our father, for he does not believe a word you say, and if you tell tales, you shall lose your life into the bargain, but be quiet and we will let you off."

The old king was still very angry with his youngest son, and thought he really meant to have taken away his life; so he called his court together

and asked what should be done, and it was settled
that he should be put to death. The prince knew
nothing of what was going on, till one day when
the king's chief huntsman went a-hunting with him,
and they were alone in the wood together, the
huntsman looked so sorrowful that the prince said,
"My friend, what is the matter with you?" "I cannot
and dare not tell you," said he. But the prince
begged hard and said, "Only say what it is, and do
not think I shall be angry, for I will forgive you."
"Alas!" said the hunstman. "The king has ordered
me to shoot you." The prince started at this, and
said, "Let me live, and I will change dresses with
you; you shall take my royal coat to show to my
father, and do you give me your shabby one."
"With all my heart," said the huntsman. "I am sure
I shall be glad to save you, for I could not have shot
you." Then he took the prince's coat, and gave him
the shabby one, and went away through the wood.

Some time after, three grand embassies came
to the old king's court, with rich gifts of gold and
precious stones for his youngest son, which were
sent from the three kings to whom he had lent his
sword and loaf of bread, to rid them of their enemy,

and feed their people. This touched the old king's
heart, and he thought his son might still be guilt-
less, and said to his court, "Oh, that my son were
still alive! How it grieves me that I had him killed!"
"He still lives," said the huntsman; "and I rejoice
that I had pity on him, and saved him, for when
the time came, I could not shoot him, but let him
go in peace and brought home his royal coat." At
this the king was overwhelmed with joy, and made
it known throughout all his kingdom, that if his
son would come back to his court, he would
forgive him.

Meanwhile the princess was eagerly waiting the
return of her deliverer, and had a road made leading
up to her palace all of shining gold; and told her
courtiers that whoever came on horseback and rode
straight up to the gate upon it, was her true lover,
and that they must let him in; but whoever rode on
one side of it, they must be sure was not the right
one, and must send him away at once.

The time soon came, when the eldest thought
he would make haste to go to the princess, and say
that he was the one who had set her free, and that
he should have her for his wife, and the kingdom

She always shook the bed well (Mother Holle)

with her. As he came before the palace and saw the golden road, he stopped to look at it, and thought to himself, "It is a pity to ride upon this beautiful road;" so he turned aside and rode on the right of it. But when he came to the gate, the guards said to him, he was not what he said he was, and must go about his business. The second prince set out soon afterwards on the same errand; and when he came to the golden road, and his horse had set one foot upon it, he stopped to look at it, and thought it very beautiful, and said to himself, "What a pity it is that anything should tread here!" Then he too turned aside and rode on the left of it. But when he came to the gate the guards said he was not the true prince, and that he too must go away.

Now when the full year was come, the third brother left the wood, where he had lain for fear of his father's anger, and set out in search of his betrothed bride. So he journeyed on, thinking of her all the way, and rode so quickly that he did not even see the golden road, but went with his horse straight over it; and as he came to the gate, it flew open, and the princess welcomed him with joy, and said he was her deliverer and should now be her husband and lord of the kingdom, and the marriage was soon kept with great feasting. When it was over, the princess told him she had heard of his father having forgiven him, and of his wish to have him home again: so he went to visit him, and told him everything, how his brothers had cheated and robbed him, and yet that he had borne all these wrongs for the love of his father. Then the old king was very angry, and wanted to punish his wicked sons; but they made their escape, and got into a ship and sailed away over the wide sea, and were never heard of any more.

THE FOUR CLEVER BROTHERS

"DEAR children," said a poor man to his four sons, "I have nothing to give you; you must go out into the world, and try your luck. Begin by learning some trade, and see how you can get on." So the four brothers took their walking sticks in their hands, and their little bundles on their shoulders, and, after bidding their father goodbye, went all out at the gate together. When they had got on some way they came to four crossways, each leading to a different country. Then the eldest said, "Here we must part; but this day four years we will come back to this spot; and in the meantime each must try what he can do for himself." So each brother went his way; and as the oldest was hastening on, a

man met him, and asked where he was going and
what he wanted. "I am going to try my luck in the
world, and should like to begin by learning some
trade," answered he. "Then," said the man, "go
with me, and I will teach you how to become the
cunningest thief that ever was." "No," said the
other, "that is not an honest calling, and what can
one look to earn by it in the end but the gallows?"
"Oh!" said the man. "You need not fear the gallows;
for I will only teach you to steal what will be fair
game; I meddle with nothing but what no one else
can get or care anything about, and where no one
can find you out." So the young man agreed to
follow his trade, and he soon showed himself so
clever that nothing could escape that he had once set
his mind upon.

The second brother also met a man, who, when
he found out what he was setting out upon, asked
him what trade he meant to learn. "I do not know
yet," said he. "Then come with me, and be a star-
gazer. It is a noble trade, for nothing can be hidden
from you when you understand the stars." The
plan pleased him much, and he soon became such a

skilful star-gazer, that when he had served out his time, and wanted to leave his master, he gave him a glass, and said, "With this you can see all that is passing in the sky and on earth, and nothing can be hidden from you."

The third brother met a huntsman, who took him with him, and taught him so well all that belonged to hunting that he became very clever in that trade; and when he left his master he gave him a bow, and said, "Whatever you shoot at with this bow you will be sure to hit."

The youngest brother likewise met a man who asked him what he wished to do. "Would not you like," said he, "to be a tailor?" "Oh no!" said the young man. "Sitting cross-legged from morning to night, working backwards and forwards with a needle and goose, will never suit me." "Oh!" answered the man. "That is not my sort of tailoring; come with me, and you will learn quite another kind of trade from that." Not knowing what better to do, he came into the plan, and learned the trade from the beginning, and when he left his master, he gave him a needle, and said, "You can sew anything with this, be it as soft as an egg, or as hard as steel, and the joint will be so fine that no seam will be seen."

After the space of four years, at the time agreed upon, the four brothers met at the four crossroads, and having welcomed each other, set off towards their father's home, where they told him all that had happened to them, and how each had learned some trade. Then one day, as they were sitting before the house under a very high tree, the father said, "I should like to try what each of you can do in his trade." So he looked up, and said to the second son, "At the top of this tree there is a chaffinch's nest; tell me how many eggs there are in it." The star-gazer took his glass, looked up, and said, "Five." "Now," said the father to the eldest son, "take away the eggs without the bird that is sitting upon them and hatching them, knowing anything of what you are doing." So the cunning thief climbed up the tree, and brought away to his father the five eggs from under the bird, who never saw or felt what he was doing, but kept sitting on at her ease. Then the father took the eggs, and put one on each corner of the table and the fifth in the middle, and said to the huntsman, "Cut all the eggs in two pieces at one shot." The huntsman took up his bow, and at one shot struck all the five eggs as his father wished. "Now comes your turn," said he to the young tailor. "Sew the eggs and the young birds in them together again, so neatly that the shot shall have done them no harm." Then the tailor took his needle and sewed the eggs as he was told; and when he had done, the thief was sent to take them back to the nest, and put them under the bird, without its knowing it. Then she went on sitting, and hatched them; and in a few days they crawled out, and had only a little red streak across their necks where the tailor had sewed them together.

"Well done, sons!" said the old man. "You have made good use of your time, and learned something worth the knowing; but I am sure I do not know which ought to have the prize. Oh, that a time might soon come for you to turn your skill to some account!"

Not long after this there was a great bustle in the country; for the king's daughter had been carried off by a mighty dragon, and the king mourned over his loss day and night, and made it

known that whoever brought her back to him
should have her for a wife. Then the four brothers
said to each other, "Here is a chance for us; let us
try what we can do." And they agreed to see
whether they could not set the princess free. "I will
soon find out where she is, however," said the star-
gazer as he looked through his glass, and soon cried
out, "I see her afar off, sitting upon a rock in the
sea, and I can spy the dragon close by, guarding
her." Then he went to the king, and asked for a
ship for himself and his brothers, and went with
them upon the sea till they came to the right place.
There they found the princess sitting, as the star-
gazer had said, on the rock, and the dragon was
lying asleep with his head upon her lap. "I dare not
shoot him," said the huntsman, "for I should kill
the beautiful young lady also." "Then I will try my
skill," said the thief; and went and stole her away
from under the dragon so quickly and gently that
the beast did not know it, but went on snoring.

Then away they hastened with her full of joy
in their boat towards the ship; but soon came the
dragon roaring behind them through the air, for he
awoke and missed the princess; but when he got

over the boat, and wanted to pounce upon them and carry off the princess, the huntsman took up his bow and shot him straight at the heart, so that he fell down dead. They were still not safe; for he was such a great beast, that in his fall he overset the boat, and they had to swim in the open sea upon a few planks. So the tailor took his needle, and with a few large stitches put some of the planks together, and sat down upon them, and sailed about and gathered up all the pieces of the boat, and tacked them together so quickly that the boat was soon ready, and they then reached the ship and got home safe.

When they had brought home the princess to her father, there was great rejoicing; and he said to the four brothers, "One of you shall marry her, but you must settle amongst yourselves which it is to be." Then there arose a quarrel between them; and the star-gazer said, "If I had not found the princess out, all your skill would have been of no use; therefore she ought to be mine." "Your seeing her would have been of no use," said the thief, "if I had not taken her away from the dragon; therefore she ought to be mine." "No, she is mine," said the huntsman; "for if I had not killed the dragon, he would after all have torn you and the princess into pieces." "And if I had not sewed the boat together again," said the tailor, "you would all have been drowned; therefore she is mine." Then the king put in a word, and said, "Each of you is right; and as all cannot have the young lady, the best way is for none of you to have her; and to make up for the loss, I will give each, as a reward for his skill, half a kingdom." So the brothers agreed that would be much better than quarrelling; and the king then gave each half a kingdom, as he had said; and they lived very happily the rest of their days, and took good care of their father.

THE SALAD

As a merry young huntsman was once going briskly along through a wood, there came up a little old woman, and said to him, "Good day, good day; you seem merry enough, but I am hungry and thirsty; do pray give me something to eat." The huntsman took pity on her, and put his hand in his pocket and gave her what he had. Then he wanted to go his way; but she took hold of him, and said, "Listen, my friend, to what I am going to tell you; I will reward you for your kindness; go your way, and after a little time you will come to a tree where you will see nine birds sitting on a cloak. Shoot into the midst of them, and one will fall down dead: the cloak will fall too; take it, it is a wishing-cloak, and when you wear it you will find yourself at any place where you may wish to be. Cut open the dead bird, take out its heart and keep it, and you will find a piece of gold under your pillow every morning when you rise. It is the bird's heart that will bring you this good luck."

The huntsman thanked her, and thought to himself, "If all this does happen, it will be a fine thing for me." When he had gone a hundred steps or so, he heard a screaming and chirping in the branches over him, and looked up and saw a flock of birds pulling a cloak with their bills and feet; screaming, fighting, and tugging at each other as if each wished to have it himself. "Well," said the huntsman, "this is wonderful; this happens just as the old woman said;" then he shot into the midst of them so that their feathers flew all about. Off went the flock chattering away; but one fell down dead, and the cloak with it. Then the huntsman did as the old woman told him, cut open the bird, took out the heart, and carried the cloak home with him.

The next morning when he awoke he lifted up his pillow, and there lay the piece of gold glittering underneath; the same happened next day, and indeed every day when he arose. He heaped up a great deal of gold, and at last thought to himself, "Of what use is this gold to me whilst I am at home? I will go out into the world and look about me."

Then he took leave of his friends, and hung his bag and bow about his neck, and went his way. It so happened that his road one day led through a thick wood, at the end of which was a large castle in a green meadow, and at one of the windows stood an old woman with a very beautiful young lady by her side looking about them. Now the old woman was a fairy, and said to the young lady, "There is a young man coming out of the wood who carries a wonderful prize; we must get it away from him, my dear child, for it is more fit for us than for him. He has a bird's heart that brings a piece of gold under his pillow every morning." Meantime the huntsman came nearer and looked at the lady, and said to himself, "I have been travelling so long that I should like to go into this castle and rest myself, for I have money enough to pay for anything I want;" but the real reason was, that he wanted to see more of the beautiful lady. Then he

went into the house, and was welcomed kindly;
and it was not long before he was so much in love
that he thought of nothing else but looking at the
lady's eyes, and doing everything that she wished.
Then the old woman said, "Now is the time for
getting the bird's heart." So the lady stole it away,
and he never found any more gold under his pillow,
for it lay now under the young lady's, and the old
woman took it away every morning; but he was so
much in love that he never missed his prize.

"Well," said the old fairy, "we have got the
bird's heart, but not the wishing-cloak yet, and that
we must also get." "Let us leave him that," said the
young lady; "he has already lost his wealth." Then
the fairy was very angry, and said, "Such a cloak is
a very rare and wonderful thing, and I must and
will have it." So she did as the old woman told her,
and set herself at the window, and looked about the
country and seemed very sorrowful; then the huntsman said, "What makes you so sad?" "Alas! dear
sir," said she, "yonder lies the granite rock where
all the costly diamonds grow, and I want so much
to go there, that whenever I think of it I cannot
help being sorrowful, for who can reach it? Only

the birds and the flies – man cannot." "If that's all your grief," said the huntsman, "I'll take you there with all my heart;" so he drew her under his cloak, and the moment he wished to be on the granite mountain they were both there. The diamonds glittered so on all sides that they were delighted with the sight and picked up the finest. But the old fairy made a deep sleep come upon him, and he said to the young lady, "Let us sit down and rest ourselves a little, I am so tired that I cannot stand any longer." So they sat down, and he laid his head in her lap and fell asleep; and whilst he was sleeping on she took the cloak from his shoulders, hung it on her own, picked up the diamonds, and wished herself home again.

When he awoke and found that his lady had tricked him, and left him alone on the wild rock, he said, "Alas! What roguery there is in the world!" and there he sat in great grief and fear, not knowing what to do. Now this rock belonged to fierce giants who lived upon it; and as he saw three of them striding about, he thought to himself, "I can only save myself by feigning to be asleep;" so he laid himself down as if he were in a sound sleep. When

the giants came up to him, the first pushed him
with his foot, and said, "What worm is this that lies
here curled up?" "Tread upon him and kill him,"
said the second. "It's not worth the trouble," said
the third. "Let him live, he'll go climbing higher
up the mountain, and some cloud will come rolling
and carry him away." And they passed on. But the
huntsman had heard all they said; and as soon as
they were gone, he climbed to the top of the
mountain, and when he had sat there a short time a
cloud came rolling around him, and caught him in
a whirlwind and bore him along for some time, till
it settled in a garden, and he fell quite gently to the
ground amongst the greens and cabbages.

Then he looked around him, and said, "I wish
I had something to eat, if not I shall be worse off
than before; for here I see neither apples nor pears,
nor any kind of fruits, nothing but vegetables." At
last he thought to himself, "I can eat salad, it will
refresh and strengthen me." So he picked out a fine
head and ate of it; but scarcely had he swallowed
two bites when he felt himself quite changed, and
saw with horror that he was turned into an ass.
However, he still felt very hungry, and the salad

The dragon came roaring through the air
(The Four Clever Brothers)

tasted very nice; so he ate on till he came to another
kind of salad, and scarcely had he tasted it when he
felt another change come over him, and soon saw
that he was lucky enough to have found his old
shape again.

Then he laid himself down and slept off a little
of his weariness; and when he awoke the next
morning he broke off a head both of the good and
the bad salad, and thought to himself, "This will
help me to my fortune again, and enable me to pay
off some folks for their treachery." So he went
away to try and find the castle of his old friends;
and after wandering about a few days he luckily
found it. Then he stained his face all over brown,
so that even his mother would not have known
him, and went into the castle and asked for a
lodging. "I am so tired," said he, "that I can go no
farther." "Countryman," said the fairy, "who are
you? And what is your business?" "I am," said he,
"a messenger sent by the king to find the finest
salad that grows under the sun. I have been lucky
enough to find it, and have brought it with me; but
the heat of the sun scorches so that it begins to
wither, and I don't know that I can carry it farther."

When the fairy and the young lady heard of this beautiful salad, they longed to taste it, and said, "Dear countryman, let us just taste it." "To be sure," answered he; "I have two heads of it with me, and will give you one;" so he opened his bag and gave them the bad. Then the fairy herself took it into the kitchen to be dressed; and when it was ready she could not wait till it was carried up, but took a few leaves immediately and put them in her mouth, and scarcely were they swallowed when she lost her own form and ran braying down into the court in the form of an ass. Now the servant maid came into the kitchen, and seeing the salad ready, was going to carry it up; but on the way she too felt a wish to taste it as the old woman had done, and ate some leaves; so she also was turned into an ass and ran after the other, letting the dish with the salad fall on the ground. The messenger sat all this time with the beautiful young lady, and as nobody came with the salad and she longed to taste it, she said, "I don't know where the salad can be." Then he thought something must have happened, and said, "I will go into the kitchen and see." And as he went he saw two asses in the court running about, and the salad lying on the ground. "All right!" said he. "Those two have had their share." Then he took up the rest of the leaves, laid them on the dish and brought them to the young lady, saying, "I bring you the dish myself that you may not wait any longer." So she ate of it, and like the others ran off into the court, braying away.

Then the huntsman washed his face and went into the court that they might know him. "Now you shall be paid for your roguery," said he; and tied them all three to a rope and took them along with him till he came to a mill and knocked at the window. "What's the matter?" said the miller. "I have three tiresome beasts here," said the other. "If you will take them, give them food and room, and treat them as I tell you, I will pay you whatever you ask." "With all my heart," said the miller; "but how shall I treat them?" Then the huntsman said, "Give the old one stripes three times a day and hay once; give the next (who was the servant-maid) stripes once a day and hay three times; and give the youngest (who was the beautiful lady) hay three times a day and no stripes:" for he could not find it in his heart to have her beaten. After this he went back to the castle, where he found everything he wanted.

Some days after the miller came to him and told him that the old ass was dead. "The other two," said he, "are alive and eat, but are so sorrowful that they cannot last long." Then the huntsman pitied them, and told the miller to drive them back to him, and when they came, he gave them some of the good salad to eat. And the beautiful young lady fell upon her knees before him, and said, "O dearest huntsman! Forgive me all the ill I have done you; my mother forced me to it, it was against my will, for I always loved you very much. Your wishing-cloak hangs up in the closet, and as for the bird's heart, I will give it you too." But he said, "Keep it, it will be just the same thing, for I mean to make you my wife." So they were married, and lived together very happily till they died.

THE FIVE SERVANTS

SOME time ago there reigned in a country many thousands of miles off, an old queen who was very spiteful and delighted in nothing so much as mischief. She had one daughter, who was thought to be the most beautiful princess in the world; but her mother only made use of her as a trap for the unwary; and whenever any suitor who had heard of her beauty came to seek her in marriage, the only answer the old lady gave to each was, that he must undertake some very hard task and forfeit his life if he failed. Many, led by the report of the princess's charms, undertook these tasks, but failed in doing what the queen set them to do. No mercy was ever shown them; but the word was given at once, and off their heads were cut.

Now it happened that a prince who lived in a country far off, heard of the great beauty of this young lady, and said to his father, "Dear father, let me go and try my luck." "No," said the king; "if you go you will surely lose your life." The prince, however, had set his heart so much upon the scheme, that when he found his father was against it he fell very ill, and took to his bed for seven years, and no art could cure him, or recover his lost spirits: so when his father saw that if he went on thus he would die, he said to him with a heart full of grief, "If it must be so, go and try your luck." At this he rose from his bed, recovered his health and spirits, and went forward on his way light of heart and full of joy.

Then on he journeyed over hill and dale, through fair weather and foul, till one day, as he was riding through a wood, he thought he saw afar off some large animal upon the ground, and as he drew near he found that it was a man lying alone upon the grass under the trees; but he looked more like a mountain than a man, he was so fat and jolly.

When this big fellow saw the traveller, he arose, and said, "If you want anyone to wait upon you, you will do well to take me into your service." "What should I do with such a fat fellow as you?" said the prince. "It would be nothing to you if I were three thousand times as fat," said the man, "so that I do but behave myself well." "That's true," answered the prince; "so come with me, I can put you to some use or another I dare say." Then the fat man rose up and followed the prince, and by and by they saw another man lying on the ground with his ear close to the turf. The prince said, "What are you doing there?" "I am listening," answered the man. "To what?" "To all that is going on in the world, for I can hear everything, I can even hear the grass grow." "Tell me," said the prince, "what you hear is going on at the court of the old queen, who has the beautiful daughter?" "I hear," said the listener, "the noise of the sword that is cutting off the head of one of her suitors." "Well!" said the prince. "I see I shall be able to make you of use; come along with me!" They had not gone far before they saw a pair of feet, and then part of the legs of a man stretched out; but they were so long that they could not see the rest of the body, till they had passed on a good deal farther, and at last they came to the body, and, after going on a while farther, to the head. "Bless me!" said the prince. "What a long rope you are!" "Oh!" answered the tall man. "This is nothing; when I choose to stretch myself to my full length, I am three times as high as any mountain you have seen on your travels, I warrant you; I will willingly do what I can to serve you if you will let me." "Come along then," said the prince. "I can turn you to account in some way."

The prince and his train went on farther into the wood, and next saw a man lying by the roadside basking in the heat of the sun, yet shaking and shivering all over, so that not a limb lay still. "What makes you shiver," said the prince, "while the sun is shining so warm?" "Alas!" answered the man. "The warmer it is, the colder I am; the sun only seems to me like a sharp frost that thrills through all my bones; and on the other hand, when others are what you call cold I begin to be warm, so that I can neither bear the ice for its heat nor the fire for its cold." "You are a queer fellow," said the prince; "but if you have nothing else to do, come along with me." The next thing they saw was a man standing, stretching his neck and looking around him from hill to hill. "What are you looking for so eagerly?" said the prince. "I have such sharp eyes," said the man, "that I can see over woods and fields and hills and dales; in short, all over the world." "Well," said the prince, "come with me if you will, for I want one more to make up my train."

Then they all journeyed on, and met with no one else till they came to the city where the beautiful princess lived. The prince went straight to the old queen, and said, "Here I am, ready to do any task you set me, if you will give your daughter as a reward when I have done." "I will set you three tasks," said the queen; "and if you get through all, you shall be the husband of my daughter. First, you must bring me a ring which I dropped in the red sea." The prince went home to his friends and said, "The first task is not an easy one; it is to fetch a ring out of the red sea, so lay your heads together and say what is to be done." Then the sharp-sighted one said, "I will see where it lies," and looked down into the sea, and cried out, "There it lies upon a rock at the bottom." "I would fetch it out," said

the tall man, "if I could but see it." "Well!" cried
out the fat one. "I will help you to do that," and
laid himself down and held his mouth to the water,
and drank up the waves till the bottom of the sea
was as dry as a meadow. Then the tall man stooped
a little and pulled out the ring with his hand, and
the prince took it to the old queen, who looked at
it, and wondering said, "It is indeed the right ring;
you have gone through this task well: but now
comes the second; look yonder at the meadow
before my palace; see! There are a hundred fat oxen
feeding there; you must eat them all up before
noon: and underneath in my cellar there are a
hundred casks of wine, which you must drink all
up." "May I not invite some guest to share the feast
with me?" said the prince. "Why, yes!" said the old
woman with a spiteful laugh. "You may ask one of
your friends to breakfast with you, but no more."

Then the prince went home and said to the fat
man, "You must be my guest today, and for once
you shall eat your fill." So the fat man set to work
and ate the hundred oxen without leaving a bit, and
asked if that was to be all he should have for his
breakfast? And he drank the wine out of the casks

without leaving a drop, licking even his fingers when he had done. When the meal was ended, the prince went to the old woman and told her the second task was done. "Your work is not all over, however," muttered the old hag to herself; "I will catch you yet, you shall not keep your head upon your shoulders if I can help it." "This evening," said she, "I will bring my daughter into your house and leave her with you; you shall sit together there, but take care that you do not fall asleep; for I shall come when the clock strikes twelve, and if she is not then with you, you are undone." "Oh!" thought the prince. "It is an easy task to keep my eyes open." So he called his servants and told them all that the old woman had said. "Who knows though," said he, "but there may be some trick at the bottom of this? It is as well to be upon our guard and keep watch that the young lady does not get away." When it was night the old woman brought her daughter to the prince's house; then the tall man twisted himself round about it, the listener put his ear to the ground, the fat man placed himself before the door so that no living soul could enter, and the sharp-eyed one looked out afar and

watched. Within sat the princess without saying a
word, but the moon shone bright through the
window upon her face, and the prince gazed upon
her wonderful beauty. And while he looked upon
her with a heart full of joy and love, his eyelids did
not droop; but at eleven o'clock the old woman
cast a charm over them so that they all fell asleep,
and the princess vanished in a moment.

And thus they slept till a quarter to twelve,
when the charm had no longer any power over
them, and they all awoke. "Alas! Alas! Woe is me,"
cried the prince; "now I am lost for ever." And his
faithful servants began to weep over their unhappy
lot; but the listener said, "Be still and I will listen;"
so he listened a while, and cried out, "I hear her
bewailing her fate;" and the sharp-sighted man
looked, and said, "I see her sitting on a rock three
hundred miles hence; now help us, my tall friend;
if you stand up, you will reach her in two steps."
"Very well," answered the tall man; and in an
instant, before one could turn one's head round, he
was at the foot of the enchanted rock. Then the tall
man took the young lady in his arms and carried
her back to the prince a moment before it struck

The tall man twisted himself about it

twelve; and they all sat down again and made merry. And when the clock struck twelve the old queen came sneaking by with a spiteful look, as if she was going to say "Now he is mine;" nor could she think otherwise, for she knew that her daughter was but the moment before on the rock three hundred miles off; but when she came and saw her daughter in the prince's room, she started, and said, "There is somebody here who can do more than I can." However, she now saw that she could no longer avoid giving the prince her daughter for a wife, but said to her in a whisper, "It is a shame that you should be won by servants, and not have a husband of your own choice."

Now the young lady was of a very proud, haughty temper, and her anger was raised to such a pitch, that the next morning she ordered three hundred loads of wood to be brought and piled up; and told the prince it was true he had by the help of his servants done the three tasks, but that before she would marry him someone must sit upon that pile of wood when it was set on fire and bear the heat. She thought to herself that though his servants had done everything else for him, none of them would go so far as to burn themselves for him, and that then she should put his love to the test by seeing whether he would sit upon it himself. But she was mistaken; for when the servants heard this, they said, "We have all done something but the frosty man; now his turn is come;" and they took him and put him on the wood and set it on fire. Then the fire rose and burned for three long days, till all the wood was gone; and when it was out, the frosty man stood in the midst of the ashes trembling like an aspen-leaf, and said, "I never shivered so much in my life; if it had lasted much longer, I should have lost the use of my limbs."

When the princess had no longer any plea for delay, she saw that she was bound to marry the prince; but when they were going to church, the old woman said, "I will never consent;" and sent secret orders out to her horsemen to kill and slay all before them and bring back her daughter before she could be married. However, the listener had pricked up his ears and heard all that the old woman said, and told it to the prince. So they made haste and got to the church first and were married; and then the five servants took their leave and went away saying, "We will go and try our luck in the world on our own account."

The prince set out with his wife, and at the end of the first day's journey came to a village, where a swineherd was feeding his swine; and as they came near he said to his wife, "Do you know who I am? I am not a prince, but a poor swineherd; he whom you see yonder with the swine is my father, and our business will be to help him to tend them." Then he went into the swineherd's hut with her, and ordered her royal clothes to be taken away in the night; so that when she awoke in the morning, she had nothing to put on, till the woman who lived there made a great favour of giving her an old gown and a pair of worsted stockings. "If it were not for your husband's sake," said she, "I would not have given you anything." Then the poor princess gave herself up for lost, and believed that her husband must indeed be a swineherd; but she thought she would make the best of it, and began to help him to feed them, and said, "It is a just reward for my pride." When this had lasted eight days she could bear it no longer, for her feet were all over wounds, and as she sat down and wept by

She ran braying into the court (The Salad)

the wayside, some people came up to her and pitied her, and asked if she knew what her husband really was. "Yes," said she; "a swineherd; he is just gone out to market with some of his stock." But they said, "Come along and we will take you to him;" and they took her over the hill to the palace of the prince's father; and when they came into the hall, there stood her husband so richly dressed in his royal clothes that she did not know him till he fell upon her neck and kissed her, and said, "I have borne much for your sake, and you too have also borne a great deal for me." Then the guests were sent for, and the marriage feast was given, and all made merry and danced and sang, and the best wish that I can wish is, that you and I had been there too.

CAT-SKIN

THERE was once a king, whose queen had hair of the purest gold, and was so beautiful that her match was not to be met with on the whole face of the earth. But this beautiful queen fell ill, and when she felt that her end drew near, she called the king to her and said, "Vow to me that you will never marry again, unless you meet with a wife who is as beautiful as I am, and who has golden hair like mine." Then when the king in his grief had vowed all she asked, she shut her eyes and died. But the king was not to be comforted, and for a long time never thought of taking another wife. At last, however, his counsellors said, "This will not do; the king must marry again, that we may have a queen." So messengers were sent far and wide, to seek for a bride who was as beautiful as the late queen. But there was no princess in the world so beautiful; and if there had been, still there was not one to be found who had such golden hair. So the messengers came home and had done all their work for nothing.

Now the king had a daughter who was just as beautiful as her mother, and had the same golden hair. And when she was grown up, the king looked at her and saw that she was just like his late queen: then he said to his courtiers, "May I not marry my daughter? She is the very image of my dead wife: unless I have her, I shall not find any bride upon the whole earth, and you say there must be a queen." When the courtiers heard this, they were shocked, and said, "Heaven forbid that a father should marry his daughter! Out of so great a sin no good can come." And his daughter was also shocked, but hoped the king would soon give up such thoughts: so she said to him, "Before I marry anyone I must have three dresses; one must be of gold like the sun, another must be of shining silver like the moon, and a third must be dazzling as the stars: besides this, I want a mantle of a thousand different kinds of fur put together, to which every beast in the kingdom must give a part of his skin." And thus she thought he would think of the matter no more. But the king made the most skilful workmen in his kingdom weave the three dresses, one as golden as the sun, another as silvery as the moon, and a third shining like the stars; and his hunters were told to hunt out all the beasts in his kingdom and take the finest fur out of their skins: and so a mantle of a thousand furs was made.

When all was ready, the king sent them to her; but she got up in the night when all were asleep, and took three of her trinkets, a golden ring, a golden necklace, and a golden brooch; and packed the three dresses of the sun, moon, and stars, up in a nutshell, and wrapped herself up in the mantle of all sorts of fur, and besmeared her face and hands with soot. Then she threw herself upon heaven for help in her need, and went away and journeyed on the whole night, till at last she came to a large wood. As she was very tired, she sat herself down in the hollow of a tree and soon fell asleep: and there she slept on till it was midday: and it happened, that as the king to whom the wood belonged was hunting in it, his dogs came to the tree, and began to sniff about and run round and round, and then to bark. "Look sharp," said the king to the huntsmen, "and see what sort of game lies there." And the huntsmen went up to the tree, and when they came back again said, "In the hollow tree there lies a most wonderful beast, such as we never saw before; its skin seems of a thousand kinds of fur, but there it lies fast asleep." "See," said the king, "if you can catch it alive, and we will take it with us." So the huntsmen took it up, and the maiden awoke and was greatly frightened, and said, "I am a poor child that has neither father nor mother left; have pity on me and take me with you." Then they said, "Yes, Miss Cat-skin, you will do for the kitchen; you can sweep up the ashes and do things of that sort." So they put her in the coach and took her home to the king's palace. Then they showed her a little corner under the staircase where no light of day ever peeped in, and said, "Cat-skin, you may lie and sleep there." And she was sent into the kitchen, and made to fetch wood and water, to blow the fire, pluck the poultry, pick the herbs, sift the ashes, and do all the dirty work.

Thus Cat-skin lived for a long time very sorrowfully. "Ah! Pretty Princess!" thought she. "What will now become of thee!" But it happened one day that a feast was to be held in the king's castle; so she said to the cook, "May I go up a little while and see what is going on? I will take care and stand behind the door." And the cook said, "Yes, you may go, but be back again in half an hour's time to rake out the ashes." Then she took her little lamp, and went into her cabin, and took off the fur skin, and washed the soot from off her face and hands, so that her beauty shone forth like the sun from behind the clouds. She next opened her nut-shell, and brought out of it the dress that shone like the sun, and so went to the feast. Everyone made way for her, for nobody knew her, and they thought she could be no less than a king's daughter. But the king came up to her and held out his hand and danced with her, and he thought in his heart, "I never saw one half so beautiful."

When the dance was at an end, she curtsied; and when the king looked round for her, she was gone, no one knew whither. The guards who stood at the castle gate were called in; but they had seen no one. The truth was, that she had run into her little cabin, pulled off her dress, blacked her face and hands, put on the fur-skin cloak, and was Cat-skin again. When she went into the kitchen to her work, and began to rake the ashes, the cook said, "Let that alone till the morning, and heat the king's soup; I should like to run up now and give a peep; but take care you don't let a hair fall into it, or you will run a chance of never eating again."

As soon as the cook went away, Cat-skin heated the king's soup and toasted up a slice of bread as nicely as ever she could; and when it was ready, she went and looked in the cabin for her little golden ring, and put it into the dish in which the soup was. When the dance was over, the king ordered his soup to be brought in, and it pleased him so well, that he thought he had never tasted any so good before. At the bottom he saw a gold ring lying, and as he could not make out how it had got there, he ordered the cook to be sent for. The cook was frightened when she heard the order, and said to Cat-skin, "You must have let a hair fall into the soup; if it be so, you will have a good beating." Then she went before the king, and he

asked her who had cooked the soup. "I did,"
answered she. But the king said, "That is not true;
it was better done than you could do it." Then she
answered, "To tell the truth, I did not cook it, but
Cat-skin did." "Then let Cat-skin come up," said
the king: and when she came, he said to her, "Who
are you?" "I am a poor child," said she, "who has
lost both father and mother." "How came you in
my palace?" asked he. "I am good for nothing,"
said she, "but to be scullion girl, and to have boots
and shoes thrown at my head." "But how did you
get the ring that was in the soup?" asked the king.
But she would not own that she knew anything
about the ring; so the king sent her away again
about her business.

After a time there was another feast, and Cat-
skin asked the cook to let her go up and see it as
before. "Yes," she said, "but come back again in
half an hour, and cook the king the soup that he
likes so much." Then she ran to her little cabin,
washed herself quickly, and took the dress out
which was silvery as the moon, and put it on; and
when she went in looking like a king's daughter,
the king went up to her and rejoiced at seeing her

again, and when the dance began, he danced with
her. After the dance was at an end, she managed to
slip out so slily that the king did not see where she
was gone; but she sprang into her little cabin and
made herself into Cat-skin again, and went into the
kitchen to cook the soup. Whilst the cook was
above, she got the golden necklace, and dropped it
into the soup; then it was brought to the king, who
ate it, and it pleased him as well as before; so he
sent for the cook, who was again forced to tell him
that Cat-skin had cooked it. Cat-skin was brought
again before the king; but she still told him that she
was only fit to have the boots and shoes thrown at
her head.

But when the king had ordered a feast to be
got ready for the third time, it happened just the
same as before. "You must be a witch, Cat-skin,"
said the cook; "for you always put something into
the soup, so that it pleases the king better than
mine." However, she let her go up as before. Then
she put on the dress which sparkled like the stars,
and went into the ballroom in it: and the king
danced with her again, and thought she had never
looked so beautiful as she did then: so whilst he

was dancing with her, he put a gold ring on her finger without her seeing it, and ordered that the dance should be kept up for a long time. When it was at an end, he would have held her fast by the hand; but she slipped away and sprang so quickly through the crowd that he lost sight of her; and she ran as fast as she could into her little cabin under the stairs. But this time she kept away too long, and stayed beyond the half-hour; so she had not time to take off her fine dress, but threw her fur mantle over it, and in her haste did not soot herself all over, but left one finger white.

Then she ran into the kitchen and cooked the king's soup; and as soon as the cook was gone, she put the golden brooch into the dish. When the king got to the bottom, he ordered Cat-skin to be called once more, and soon saw the white finger and the ring that he had put on it whilst they were dancing: so he seized her hand, and kept fast hold of it, and when she wanted to loose herself and spring away, the fur cloak fell off a little on one side, and the starry dress sparkled underneath it. Then he got hold of the fur and tore it off, and her golden hair and beautiful form were seen, and she could no

longer hide herself: so she washed the soot and
ashes from off her face, and showed herself to be
the most beautiful princess upon the face of the
earth. But the king said, "You are my beloved
bride, and we will never more be parted from each
other." And the wedding feast was held, and a
merry day it was.

THE ROBBER-BRIDEGROOM

THERE was once a miller who had a pretty daughter; and when she was grown up, he thought to himself, "If a seemly man should come to ask her for his wife, I will give her to him that she may be taken care of." Now it so happened that one did come, who seemed to be very rich, and behaved very well; and as the miller saw no reason to find fault with him, he said he should have his daughter. Yet the maiden did not love him quite so well as a bride ought to love her bridegroom, but, on the other hand, soon began to feel a kind of inward shuddering whenever she saw or thought of him.

One day he said to her, "Why do you not come and see my home, since you are to be my bride?" "I

do not know where your house is," said the girl.
"'Tis out there," said her bridegroom, "yonder in the
dark green wood." Then she began to try and avoid
going, and said, "But I cannot find the way thither."
"Well, but you must come and see me next Sunday,"
said the bridegroom. "I have asked some guests to
meet you, and that you may find your way through
the wood, I will strew ashes for you along the path."

When Sunday came and the maiden was to go
out, she felt very much troubled, and took care to
put on two pockets, and filled them with peas and
beans. She soon came to the wood, and found her
path strewed with ashes; so she followed the track,
and at every step threw a pea on the right and a
bean on the left side of the road; and thus she
journeyed on the whole day till she came to a house
which stood in the middle of the dark wood. She
saw no one within, and all was quite still, till on a
sudden she heard a voice cry,

> "Turn again, bonny bride!
>   Turn again home!
> Haste from the robber's den,
>   Haste away home!"

She looked around, and saw a little bird sitting in a cage that hung over the door; and he flapped his wings, and again she heard him cry,

> "Turn again, bonny bride!
>   Turn again home!
>   Haste from the robber's den,
>   Haste away home!"

However, the bride went in, and roamed along from one room to another, and so over all the house; but it was quite empty, and not a soul could she see. At last she came to a room where a very very old woman was sitting. "Pray, can you tell me, my good woman," said she, "if my bridegroom lives here?" "Ah! My dear child!" said the old woman. "You are come to fall into the trap laid for you: your wedding can only be with Death, for the robber will surely take away your life; if I do not save you, you are lost!" So she hid the bride behind a large cask, and then said to her, "Do not stir or move yourself at all, lest some harm should befall you; and when the robbers are asleep we will run off; I have long wished to get away."

She had hardly done this when the robbers

came in, and brought another young maiden with them who had been ensnared like the bride. Then they began to feast and drink, and were deaf to her shrieks and groans: and they gave her some wine to drink, three glasses, one of white, one of red, and one of yellow; upon which she fainted and fell down dead. Now the bride began to grow very uneasy behind the cask, and thought that she too must die in her turn. Then the one that was to be her bridegroom saw that there was a gold ring on the little finger of the maiden they had murdered; and as he tried to snatch it off, it flew up in the air and fell down again behind the cask just in the bride's lap. So he took a light and searched about all round the room for it, but could not find anything; and another of the robbers said, "Have you looked behind the large cask yet?" "Pshaw!" said the old woman. "Come, sit still and eat your supper now, and leave the ring alone till tomorrow; it won't run away, I'll warrant."

So the robbers gave up the search, and went on with their eating and drinking; but the old woman dropped a sleeping-draught into their wine, and they laid themselves down and slept, and snored roundly. And when the bride heard this, she stepped out from behind the cask; and as she was forced to walk over the sleepers, who were lying about on the floor, she trembled lest she should awaken some of them. But heaven aided her, so that she soon got through her danger; and the old woman went upstairs with her, and they both ran away from the murderous den. The ashes that had been strewed were now all blown away, but the peas and beans had taken root and were springing up, and showed her the way by the light of the moon. So they walked the whole night, and in the morning reached the mill; when the bride told her father all that had happened to her.

As soon as the day arrived when the wedding was to take place, the bridegroom came; and the miller gave orders that all his friends and relations should be asked to the feast. And as they were all sitting at table, one of them proposed that each of the guests should tell some tale. Then the bridegroom said to the bride, when it came to her turn, "Well, my dear, do you know nothing? Come, tell us some story." "Yes," answered she, "I can tell you a dream that I dreamt. I once thought I was

She got up when all were asleep (Cat-Skin)

going through a wood, and went on and on till I came to a house where there was not a soul to be seen, but a bird in a cage, that cried out twice,

> "Turn again, bonny bride!
>   Turn again home!
> Haste from the robber's den,
>   Haste away home!"

– I only dreamt that, my love. Then I went through all the rooms which were quite empty, until I came to a room where there sat a very old woman; and I said to her, 'Does my bridegroom live here?' but she answered, 'Ah! My dear child! You have fallen into a murderer's snare; your bridegroom will surely kill you;' – I only dreamt that, my love. But she hid me behind a large cask; and hardly had she done this, when the robbers came in, dragging a young woman along with them; then they gave her three kinds of wine to drink, white, red, and yellow, till she fell dead upon the ground; – I only dreamt that, my love. After they had done this, one of the robbers saw that there was a gold ring on her little finger, and snatched at it; but it flew up to the ceiling, and then fell behind the great cask just

where I was, and into my lap; and here is the ring!"
At these words she brought out the ring and
showed it to the guests.

When the robber saw all this, and heard what
she said, he grew as pale as ashes with fright, and
wanted to run off; but the guests held him fast and
gave him up to justice, so that he and all his gang
met with the due reward of their wickedness.

ROLAND AND MAY-BIRD

THERE was once a poor man who went every day to cut wood in the forest. One day as he went along he heard a cry like a little child's; so he followed the sound till at last he looked up a high tree, and on one of the branches sat a very little girl. Its mother had fallen asleep, and a vulture had taken it out of her lap and flown away with it and left it on the tree. Then the woodcutter climbed up, took the little child down, and said to himself, "I will take this poor child home and bring it up with my own son Roland." So he brought it to his cottage, and both grew up together! And he called the little girl May-bird, because he had found her on a tree in May; and May-bird and Roland were so very fond of each other that they were never happy but when they were together.

But the woodcutter became very poor, and had nothing in the world he could call his own, and indeed he had scarcely bread enough for his wife and the two children to eat. At last the time came when even that was all gone, and he knew not where to seek for help in his need. Then at night, as he lay on his bed and turned himself here and there, restless and full of care, his wife said to him, "Husband, listen to me, and take the two children out early tomorrow morning; give each of them a piece of bread, and then lead them into the midst of the wood where it is thickest, make a fire for them, and go away and leave them alone to shift for themselves, for we can no longer keep them here." "No, wife," said the husband, "I cannot find it in my heart to leave the children to the wild beasts of the forest, who would soon tear them to pieces." "Well, if you will not do as I say," answered the wife, "we must starve together:" and she let him have no peace until he came into her plan.

Meantime the poor children too were lying awake restless, and weak from hunger, so that they heard all that their mother said to her husband. "Now," thought May-bird to herself, "it is all up with us:" and she began to weep. But Roland crept to her bedside, and said, "Do not be afraid, May-bird, I will find out some help for us." Then he got up, put on his jacket, and opened the door and went out.

The moon shone bright upon the little court before the cottage, and the white pebbles glittered like daisies on the green meadows. So he stooped down, and put as many as he could into his pocket, and then went back to the house. "Now May-bird," said he, "rest in peace;" and he went to bed and fell fast asleep.

Early in the morning before the sun had risen, the woodman's wife came and awoke them. "Get up, children," said she, "we are going into the wood; there is a piece of bread for each of you, but take care of it and keep some for the afternoon." May-bird took the bread and carried it in her apron, because Roland had his pocket full of stones, and they made their way into the wood.

After they had walked on for a time, Roland stood still and looked towards home, and after a

while turned again, and so on several times. Then
his father said, "Roland, why do you keep turning
and lagging about so? Move your legs on a little
faster." "Ah! Father," answered Roland, "I am
stopping to look at my white cat that sits on the
roof, and wants to say goodbye to me." "You little
fool!" said his mother. "That is not your cat; 'tis
the morning sun shining on the chimney top."
Now Roland had not been looking at the cat, but
had all the while been staying behind to drop from
his pocket one white pebble after another along the
road.

When they came into the midst of the wood,
the woodman said, "Run about, children, and pick
up some wood, and I will make a fire to keep us all
warm." So they piled up a little heap of brushwood,
and set it a-fire; and as the flame burned bright, the
mother said, "Now set yourselves by the fire and
go to sleep, while we go and cut wood in the forest;
be sure you wait till we come again and fetch you."
Roland and May-bird sat by the fireside till the
afternoon, and then each of them ate their piece of
bread. They fancied the woodman was still in the
wood, because they thought they heard the blows

of his axe; but it was a bough which he had cunningly hung upon a tree, so that the wind blew it backwards and forwards, and it sounded like the axe as it hit the other boughs. Thus they waited till evening; but the woodman and his wife kept away, and no one came to fetch them.

When it was quite dark May-bird began to cry; but Roland said, "Wait awhile till the moon rises." And when the moon rose, he took her by the hand, and there lay the pebbles along the ground, glittering like new pieces of money, and marked the way out. Towards morning they came again to the woodman's house, and he was glad in his heart when he saw the children again; for he had grieved at leaving them alone. His wife also seemed to be glad; but in her heart she was angry at it.

Not long after there was again no bread in the house, and May-bird and Roland heard the wife say to her husband, "The children found their way back once, and I took it in good part; but there is only half a loaf of bread left for them in the house; tomorrow you must take them deeper into the wood, that they may not find their way out, or we shall all be starved." It grieved the husband in his

heart to do as his wife wished, and he thought it
would be better to share their last morsel with the
children; but as he had done as she said once, he did
not dare to say no. When the children had heard all
their plan, Roland got up and wanted to pick up
pebbles as before; but when he came to the door he
found his mother had locked it. Still he comforted
May-bird, and said, "Sleep in peace, dear May-
bird; God is very kind and will help us." Early in
the morning a piece of bread was given to each of
them, but still smaller than the one they had before.
Upon the road Roland crumbled his in his pocket,
and often stood still, and threw a crumb upon the
ground. "Why do you lag so behind, Roland?" said
the woodman. "Go your ways on before." "I am
looking at my little dove that is sitting upon the
roof and wants to say goodbye to me." "You silly
boy!" said the wife. "That is not your little dove, it
is the morning sun that shines on the chimney top."
But Roland went on crumbling his bread, and
throwing it on the ground. And thus they went on
still farther into the wood, where they had never
been before in all their life. There they were again
told to sit down by a large fire, and sleep; and the

woodman and his wife said they would come in the evening and fetch them away. In the afternoon Roland shared May-bird's bread because he had strewed all his upon the road; but the day passed away, and evening passed away too, and no one came to the poor children. Still Roland comforted May-bird, and said, "Wait till the moon rises; then I shall see the crumbs of bread which I have strewed, and they will show us the way home."

The moon rose; but when Roland looked for the crumbs, they were gone; for thousands of little birds in the wood had found them and picked them up. Roland, however, set out to try and find his way home; but they soon lost themselves in the wilderness, and went on through the night and all the next day, till at last they lay down and fell asleep for weariness: and another day they went on as before, but still did not reach the end of the wood, and were as hungry as could be, for they had nothing to eat.

In the afternoon of the third day they came to a strange little hut, made of bread, with a roof of cake, and windows of sparkling sugar. "Now we will sit down and eat till we have had enough," said

Roland; "I will eat off the roof for my share; do you eat the windows, May-bird, they will be nice and sweet for you." Whilst May-bird, however, was picking at the sugar, a sweet pretty voice called from within:

"Tip, tap! who goes there?"

But the children answered;

"The wind, the wind,
That blows through the air;"

and went on eating; and May-bird broke out a round pane of the window for herself, and Roland tore off a large piece of cake from the roof, when the door opened, and a little old fairy came gliding out. At this May-bird and Roland were so frightened, that they let fall what they had in their hands. But the old lady shook her head, and said, "Dear children, where have you been wandering about? Come in with me; you shall have something good." So she took them both by the hand, and led them into her little hut, and brought out plenty to eat, milk and pancakes, with sugar, apples, and nuts; and then two beautiful little beds were got ready, and May-bird and Roland laid themselves down, and thought they were in heaven: but the fairy was a spiteful one, and had made her pretty sweetmeat house to entrap little children. Early in the morning, before they were awake, she went to their little beds, and when she saw the two sleeping and looking so sweetly, she had no pity on them, but was glad they were in her power. Then she took up Roland, and put him in a little coop by himself; and when he awoke, he found himself behind a grating, shut up as little chickens are: but she shook May-bird, and called out, "Get up, you lazy little thing, and fetch some water; and go into the kitchen and cook something good to eat; your brother is shut up yonder; I shall first fatten him, and when he is fat, I think I shall eat him."

When the fairy was gone, the little girl watched her time and got up and ran to Roland, and told him what she had heard, and said, "We must run away quickly, for the old woman is a bad fairy, and will kill us." But Roland said, "You must first steal away her fairy wand, that we may save ourselves, if she should follow." Then the little maiden ran back, and fetched the magic wand, and away they went together; so when the old fairy came back, she could see no one at home, and sprang in a great rage to the window, and looked out into the wide world (which she could do far and near), and a long way off she spied May-bird running away with her dear Roland. "You are already a great way off," said she; "but you will still fall into my hands." Then she put on her boots, which walked several miles at a step, and scarcely made two steps with them, before she overtook the children: but May-bird saw that the fairy was coming after them, and by the help of the wand turned her dear Roland into a lake, and herself into a swan which swam about in the middle of it. So the fairy set herself down on the shore and took a great deal of trouble to decoy the swan, and threw crumbs of bread to it; but it would not come near her, and she was forced to go home in the evening, without taking her revenge. And May-bird changed herself and her dear Roland back into their own forms once more, and they went journeying on the whole night until the dawn of day; and then the maiden turned herself into a beautiful rose, which grew in the midst of a quickset hedge, and Roland sat by the side and played upon his flute.

The fairy soon came striding along. "Good piper," said she, "may I pluck the beautiful rose for myself?" "Oh yes," answered he; "and I will play to you meantime." So when she had crept into the hedge in a great hurry to gather the flower (for she well knew what it was), he began to play upon his flute; and, whether she liked it or not, such was the wonderful power of the music that she was forced to dance a merry jig, on and on without any rest. And as he did not cease playing a moment, the thorns at length tore the clothes from off her body, and pricked her sorely, and there she stuck quite fast.

Then May-bird was free once more; but she was very tired and Roland said, "Now I will hasten home for help and by and by we will be married." And May-bird said, "I will stay here in the meantime and wait for you; and, that no one may know me, I will turn myself into a stone and lie in the corner of yonder field." Then Roland went away, and May-bird was to wait for him. But Roland met

She was forced to dance a merry jig

with another maiden, who pleased him so much
that he stopped where she lived, and forgot his
former friend; and when May-bird had stayed in
the field a long time, and found he did not come
back, she became quite sorrowful, and turned herself into a little daisy, and thought to herself,
"Someone will come and tread me under foot, and
so my sorrows will end." But it so happened that
as a shepherd was keeping watch in the field he
found the flower, and thinking it very pretty, took
it home, placed it in a box in his room, and said, "I
have never found so pretty a flower before." From
that time everything throve wonderfully at the
shepherd's house: when he got up in the morning,
all the household work was ready done; the room
was swept and cleaned; the fire made, and the water
fetched: and in the afternoon, when he came home,
the tablecloth was laid and a good dinner ready set
for him. He could not make out how all this
happened; for he saw no one in his house: and
although it pleased him well enough, he was at
length troubled to think how it could be, and went
to a cunning woman who lived hard by, and asked
her what he should do. She said, "There must be

witchcraft in it; look out tomorrow morning early, and see if anything stirs about in the room; if it does, throw a white cloth at once over it, and then the witchcraft will be stopped." The shepherd did as she said, and the next morning saw the box open and the daisy come out: then he sprang up quickly and threw a white cloth over it: in an instant the spell was broken, and May-bird stood before him; for it was she who had taken care of his house for him; and as she was so beautiful he asked her if she would marry him. She said "No," because she wished to be faithful to her dear Roland; but she agreed to stay and keep house for him.

Time passed on, and Roland was to be married to the maiden that he had found; and according to an old custom in that land, all the maidens were to come and sing songs in praise of the bride and bridegroom. But May-bird was so grieved when she heard that her dearest Roland had forgotten her, and was to be married to another, that her heart seemed as if it would burst within her, and she would not go for a long time. At length she was forced to go with the rest; but she kept hiding herself behind the others until she was left the last.

Then she could not any longer help coming forward; and the moment she began to sing, Roland sprang up, and cried out, "That is the true bride; I will have no other but her;" for he knew her by the sound of her voice; and all that he had forgotten came back into his mind, and his heart was opened towards her. So faithful May-bird was married to her dear Roland, and there was an end of her sorrows; and from that time forward she lived happily till she died.

THE JUNIPER TREE

A LONG while ago, perhaps as much as two thousand years, there was a rich man who had a wife of whom he was very fond; but they had no children. Now in the garden before the house where they lived there stood a juniper tree; and one winter's day as the lady was standing under the juniper tree, paring an apple, she cut her finger, and the drops of blood trickled down upon the snow. "Ah!" said she, sighing deeply and looking down upon the blood. "How happy should I be if I had a little child as white as snow and as red as blood!" And as she was saying this, she grew quite cheerful, and was sure her wish would be fulfilled. And after a little time the snow went away, and soon afterwards the fields began to look green. Next the spring came, and the meadows were dressed with flowers; the trees put forth their green leaves; the young branches shed their blossoms upon the ground; and the little birds sang through the groves. And then came summer, and the sweet-smelling flowers of the juniper tree began to unfold; and the lady's heart leaped within her, and she fell on her knees for joy. But when autumn drew near, the fruit was thick upon the trees. Then the lady plucked the red berries from the juniper tree, and looked sad and sorrowful; and she called her husband to her, and said, "If I die, bury me under the juniper tree." Not long after this a pretty little child was born; it was, as the lady wished, as red as blood, and as white as snow; and as soon as she had looked upon it, her joy overcame her, and she fainted away and died.

Then her husband buried her under the juniper tree, and wept and mourned over her; but after a little while he grew better, and at length dried up his tears, and married another wife.

Time passed on, and he had a daughter born; but the child of his first wife, that was as red as blood, and as white as snow, was a little boy. The

mother loved her daughter very much, but hated
the little boy, and bethought herself how she might
get all her husband's money for her own child; so
she used the poor fellow very harshly, and was
always pushing him about from one corner of the
house to another, and thumping him one while and
pinching him another, so that he was for ever in
fear of her, and when he came home from school,
could never find a place in the house to play in.

Now it happened that once when the mother
was going into her storeroom, the little girl came
up to her, and said, "Mother, may I have an apple?"
"Yes, my dear," said she, and gave her a nice rosy
apple out of the chest. Now you must know that
this chest had a very thick heavy lid, with a great
sharp iron lock upon it. "Mother," said the little
girl, "pray give me one for my little brother too."
Her mother did not much like this; however, she
said, "Yes, my child; when he comes from school,
he shall have one too." As she was speaking, she
looked out of the window and saw the little boy
coming; so she took the apple from her daughter,
and threw it back into the chest and shut the lid,
telling her that she should have it again when her

brother came home. When the little boy came to the door, this wicked woman said to him with a kind voice, "Come in, my dear, and I will give you an apple." "How kind you are, mother!" said the little boy. "I should like to have an apple very much." "Well, come with me then," said she. So she took him into the storeroom and lifted up the cover of the chest, and said, "There, take one out yourself;" and then, as the little boy stooped down to reach one of the apples out of the chest, bang! She let the lid fall, so hard that his head fell off amongst the apples. When she found what she had done, she was very much frightened, and did not know how she should get the blame off her shoulders. However, she went into her bedroom, and took a white handkerchief out of a drawer, and then fitted the little boy's head upon his neck and tied the handkerchief round it, so that no one could see what had happened, and seated him on a stool before the door with the apple in his hand.

Soon afterwards Margery came into the kitchen to her mother, who was standing by the fire, and stirring about some hot water in a pot. "Mother," said Margery, "my brother is sitting before the door with an apple in his hand; I asked him to give it me, but he did not say a word, and looked so pale, that I was quite frightened." "Nonsense!" said her mother. "Go back again, and if he won't answer you, give him a good box on the ear." Margery went back, and said, "Brother, give me that apple." But he answered not a word; so she gave him a box on the ear; and immediately his head fell off. At this, you may be sure she was sadly frightened, and ran screaming out to her mother, that she had knocked off her brother's head, and cried as if her heart would break. "O Margery!" said her mother. "What have you been doing? However, what is done cannot be undone; so we had better put him out of the way, and say nothing to anyone about it."

When the father came home to dinner, he said, "Where is my little boy?" And his wife said nothing, but put a large dish of black soup upon the table; and Margery wept bitterly all the time, and could not hold up her head. And the father asked after his little boy again. "Oh!" said his wife. "I should think he is gone to his uncle's." "What business could he have to go away without bidding me goodbye?"

said his father. "I know he wished very much to go," said the woman; "and begged me to let him stay there some time; he will be well taken care of there." "Ah!" said the father, "I don't like that; he ought not to have gone away without wishing me goodbye." And with that he began to eat; but he seemed still sorrowful about his son, and said, "Margery, what do you cry so for? Your brother will come back again, I hope." But Margery by and by slipped out of the room and went to her drawers and took her best silk handkerchief out of them, and tying it round her little brother's bones, carried them out of the house weeping bitterly all the while, and laid them under the juniper tree; and as soon as she had done this, her heart felt lighter, and she left off crying. Then the juniper tree began to move itself backwards and forwards, and to stretch its branches out, one from another, and then bring them together again, just like a person clapping hands for joy: and after this, a kind of cloud came from the tree, and in the middle of the cloud was a burning fire, and out of the fire came a pretty bird, that flew away into the air, singing merrily. And as soon as the bird was gone, the handkerchief and the little boy were gone too, and the tree looked just as it had done before; but Margery felt quite happy and joyful within herself, just as if she had known that her brother had been alive again, and went into the house and ate her dinner.

But the bird flew away, and perched upon the roof of a goldsmith's house, and sang,

> "My mother slew her little son;
> My father thought me lost and gone:
> But pretty Margery pitied me,
> And laid me under the juniper tree;
> And now I rove so merrily,
> As over the hills and dales I fly:
>   O what a fine bird am I!"

The goldsmith was sitting in his shop finishing a gold chain; and when he heard the bird singing on the house-top, he started up so suddenly that one of his shoes slipped off; however, without stopping to put it on again, he ran out into the street with his apron on, holding his pincers in one hand, and the gold chain in the other. And when he saw the bird sitting on the roof with the sun shining on its bright feathers, he said, "How sweetly you sing, my pretty

bird! Pray sing that song again." "No," said the
bird, "I can't sing twice for nothing; if you will give
me that gold chain, I'll try what I can do." "There,"
said the goldsmith, "take the chain, only pray sing
that song again." So the bird flew down, and taking
the chain in its right claw, perched a little nearer to
the goldsmith, and sang:

> "My mother slew her little son;
> My father thought me lost and gone:
> But pretty Margery pitied me,
> And laid me under the juniper tree;
> And now I rove so merrily,
> As over the hills and dales I fly:
>   O what a fine bird am I!"

After that the bird flew away to a shoemaker's,
and sitting upon the roof of the house, sang the
same song as it had done before.

When the shoemaker heard the song, he ran to
the door without his coat, and looked up to the top
of the house; but he was obliged to hold his hand
before his eyes, because the sun shone so brightly.
"Bird," said he, "how sweetly you sing!" Then he
called into the house, "Wife! Wife! Come out here,

and see what a pretty bird is singing on the top of
our house!" And he called out his children and
workmen; and they all ran out and stood gazing at
the bird, with its beautiful red and green feathers,
and the bright golden ring about its neck, and eyes
which glittered like the stars. "O bird!" said the
shoemaker. "Pray sing that song again." "No," said
the bird, "I cannot sing twice for nothing; you must
give me something if I do." "Wife," said the
shoemaker, "run upstairs into the workshop, and
bring me down the best pair of new red shoes you
can find." So his wife ran and fetched them. "Here,
my pretty bird," said the shoemaker, "take these
shoes; but pray sing that song again." The bird
came down, and taking the shoes in his left claw,
flew up again to the housetop, and sang:

> "My mother slew her little son;
> My father thought me lost and gone:
> But pretty Margery pitied me,
> And laid me under the juniper tree;
> And now I rove so merrily,
> As over the hills and dales I fly:
> O what a fine bird am I!"

And when he had done singing, he flew away, holding the shoes in one claw and the chain in the other. And he flew a long, long way off, till at last he came to a mill. The mill was going clipper! clapper! clipper! clapper! and in the mill were twenty millers, who were all hard at work hewing a millstone; and the millers hewed, hick! hack! hick! hack! And the mill went on, clipper! clapper! clipper! clapper!

So the bird perched upon a linden tree by the mill, and began its song:

> "My mother slew her little son;
> My father thought me lost and gone:'

here two of the millers left off their work and listened:

> "But pretty Margery pitied me,
> And laid me under the juniper tree;"

now all the millers but one looked up and left their work;

> "And now I rove so merrily,
> As over the hills and dales I fly:
> O what a fine bird am I!"

Just as the song was ended, the last miller heard it, and started up, and said, "O bird! How sweetly you sing! Do let me hear the whole of that song; pray, sing it again!" "No," said the bird, "I cannot sing twice for nothing; give me that millstone, and I'll sing again." "Why," said the man, "the millstone does not belong to me; if it was all mine, you should have it and welcome." "Come," said the other millers, "if he will only sing that song again, he shall have the millstone." Then the bird came down from the tree: and the twenty millers fetched long poles and worked and worked heave, ho! heave, ho! till at last they raised the millstone on its side; and then the bird put its head through the hole in the middle of it, and flew away to the linden tree, and sang the same song as it had done before.

And when he had done, he spread his wings, and with the chain in one claw, and the shoes in the other, and the millstone about his neck, he flew away to his father's house.

Now it happened that his father and mother and Margery were sitting together at dinner. His father was saying, "How light and cheerful I am!"

But his mother said, "Oh, I am so heavy and so sad, I feel just as if a great storm was coming on." And Margery said nothing, but sat and cried. Just then the bird came flying along, and perched upon the top of the house. "Bless me!" said the father. "How cheerful I am; I feel as if I was about to see an old friend again." "Alas!" said the mother. "I am so sad, and my teeth chatter so, and yet it seems as if my blood was all on fire in my veins!" And she tore open her gown to cool herself. And Margery sat by herself in a corner, with her plate on her lap before her, and wept so bitterly that she cried her plate quite full of tears.

And the bird flew to the top of the juniper tree and sang:

"My mother slew her little son;"

Then the mother held her ears with her hands, and shut her eyes close, that she might neither see nor hear; but there was a sound in her ears like a frightful storm, and her eyes burned and glared like lightning. "O wife!" said the father.

"My father thought me lost and gone:"

"What a beautiful bird that is, and how finely he sings; and his feathers glitter in the sun like so many spangles!"

> "But pretty Margery pitied me,
> And laid me under the juniper tree;"

At this Margery lifted up her head and sobbed sadly, and her father said, "I must go out, and look at that bird a little nearer." "Oh! Don't leave me alone," said his wife; "I feel just as if the house was burning." However, he would go out to look at the bird; and it went on singing:

> "But now I rove so merrily,
> As over the hills and dales I fly:
> O what a fine bird am I!"

As soon as the bird had done singing, he let fall the gold chain upon his father's neck, and it fitted so nicely that he went back into the house and said, "Look here, what a beautiful chain the bird has given me; only see how grand it is!" But his wife was so frightened that she fell all along on the floor, so that her cap flew off, and she lay as if she were dead. And when the bird began singing again,

Margery said, "I must go out and see whether the bird has not something to give me." And just as she was going out of the door, the bird let fall the red shoes before her; and when she had put on the shoes, she all at once became quite light and happy, and jumped into the house and said, "I was so heavy and sad when I went out, and now I'm so happy! See what fine shoes the bird has given me!" Then the mother said, "Well, if the world should fall to pieces, I must go out and try whether I shall not be better in the air." And as she was going out, the bird let fall the millstone upon her head and crushed her to pieces.

The father and Margery hearing the noise ran out, and saw nothing but smoke and fire and flame rising up from the place; and when this was past and gone, there stood the little boy beside them; and he took his father and Margery by the hand, and they went into the house, and ate their dinner together very happily.